HER LOYAL SEAL

MIDNIGHT DELTA SERIES, BOOK 2

CAITLYN O'LEARY

PASSIONATELY KIND PUBLISHING INC.

Keep up with Caitlyn and sign up for her newsletter:

http://bit.ly/1WIhRup

To all of our men and women who have served.

SYNOPSIS

Kidnapped and Nearly Broken

Lydia Hidalgo is still defiant as she and her family are sentenced to death at the hands of the Mexican drug cartel. Not knowing if she will survive, her one request is that her sister will be cared for.

A Daring Rescue

Clint Archer and his team mates will stop at nothing to rescue Lydia and her family from their captors. Having to carry this brave woman for five days through the jungle creates a bond that he cannot resist.

Clinging to Life

The closer they got to civilization, the slimmer Lydia's chance of survival becomes. The Midnight Delta SEAL team work desperately to get her the help she needs, while Clint finds himself losing his heart more each day.

1

—————

HIS KNIFE WAS WET WITH BLOOD AS HE FOLLOWED DARIUS into the shack in the middle of the Mexican jungle. His team mate, who was the medic went straight to the woman who was tied spread-eagle to the wall. Her dress was ripped, and exposed her back. There was a bullwhip lying beside one of the dead men. He also saw another man who had a cell phone gripped in his hand. Clint grabbed it, sure it was set to film the torture of the girl.

Shrill screams broke through the room as the gag was taken out of the young woman's mouth.

"She needs to stop, but I don't want to gag her again," Darius said helplessly, as he motioned to Clint. Darius didn't speak Spanish, but he knew he did. Clint rushed over.

"She's screaming for her family. Work with the others to get them cut loose." Clint turned to his other team mates who were with an older couple and another young woman. He wiped off his knife on his fatigues and slid it carefully between the exposed wood of the wall and her wrists. God, she was a mess. He couldn't believe how deep the lacerations were from where she had struggled against the rough rope.

"Shhhh. I know you can't see them, but your family is safe," he assured her in Spanish.

"Let me see them. Papa! Mama! Beth!" Tears dripped down her face. Clint went to her other wrist and began to carefully cut it loose as well. She struggled to turn around.

"Mama!"

"Miss, you need to calm down so I can get your other hand free." Clint didn't think she heard him, she had to be out of her mind with pain. Despite that, her entire focus was on her family.

"Where are they?" She yanked so hard against the rope he didn't have any other choice but to hold her hand down so he could ensure he didn't cut her as he sliced through the rope. His fingers were slick with blood by the time he was done.

"Darius, get back here, she needs medical attention, stat!"

"We need to get out of here," Mason Gault said. Clint acknowledged his leader's words, but continued to concentrate on the woman's wounds.

"What's your name?"

"Let me go to my family?"

"Stay there. Let them help you." The older man crouched in front of her as Clint gently helped her to the floor of the cabin.

"I'm so sorry daughter this is all my fault. Oh God, I'll never be able to forgive myself." The man started weeping.

Lydia, reached out to her father, but hissed in pain.

"Enough!" Clint commanded. "This isn't helping your daughter. We have to get the hell out of here."

"Let me hold her. I'll carry her." Her father's voice trembled. Clint looked up and saw he was now surrounded by the small family. Looking at the father, he knew there wasn't a chance in hell the man would be able to carry his daughter the miles they needed to walk.

"One of my men is going to carry her," Mason said as he stalked across the room. "We need to leave here immediately. Our intel says the other members of the cartel will be here shortly."

Clint felt Lydia jerk.

"It's okay," he told her in Spanish. "Nobody is going to hurt you again, I promise."

"Just help my family," she answered in English. "Please."

"I'm going to help you. My team will help your family."

"Ms. Hidalgo, I'm going to give you something for the pain. It's not going to knock you out, because we need you to remain conscious, but it will make you feel better. I'm also going to give you some antibiotics. As soon as we're far enough away from here to be safe, I'm going to do some triage on your wounds."

"Lydia, he's going to need to give you the shot in your hip. We just need to lift your skirt just a little, okay?" She looked up at him with a pleading look.

"Can't you give me the shot in my arm?"

"No. Darius is our medic. He'll do it quickly." He so wanted to preserve her modesty, but they needed to get the medicine into her system.

She bit her lip so hard he thought she might draw blood. "All right."

Darius had it done and over with in a moment.

Clint helped her to stand, but he had to take most of

her weight. He looked over at his friend Darius, and saw the same look of resignation. They could arrange for some kind of travois, but pulling it through the jungle would slow them all down. What's more, it would be too painful on her back. Even though the medicine wasn't meant to put her to sleep, she would likely pass out from the pain. Clint hated the idea, but he was going to have to secure her to him as he carried her.

"If we tie her upper arms and wind the rope around your waist, it should support her if she lets go." Darius said, reading his mind.

He felt her shudder. "Are you talking about tying me up again?"

"Honey, do you think you're strong enough to hold onto me while I carry you miles through the jungle?" He looked into her eyes and could clearly see her struggle.

"I want to say yes, but I know I'm not." She choked back a sob. "But I can't stand the idea of being tied down again. Of not being able to get free. I just can't."

Lydia would have collapsed if Clint hadn't caught her. She let out a broken cry. He didn't blame her. She still had to be in unimaginable pain and totally freaked out about being restrained again. He had an idea.

"I'll give you one of my knives. You'll be able to cut yourself loose at any time."

"Are you out of your fucking mind?" Darius asked.

"Shut up Dare." He glared at the other man. Clint totally understood Lydia's need for control. He highly doubted the beating was the only thing she had endured.

"Once we get away from here, you're going to have to check all of them out. It's likely they have more injuries."

"I wasn't raped," Lydia said baldly.

"How about–"

"Neither was my sister. Those fucking assholes were going to, but I made them mad. That's why they started to whip me."

"Fuck."

"It doesn't matter. What's important was Beth. I hope you killed them slowly."

"Not slow enough," Darius said.

"Will you be able to hold onto me if we lift you onto my back?" Clint asked.

She hissed in pain as Darius ripped the remaining tatters of her dress off her back and used some disinfectant wipes on the wounds. More tears filled her soft brown eyes. He saw Darius pull out some antiseptic. When she tried to look backwards to see what his friend was doing to her back, he grasped her fingertips with one hand and gently turned her head to face him.

"Lydia, can you hold onto me?" he asked again.

"I'll try."

"So you understand why we need to strap you on so that you won't fall. Lydia, there is no way I'm going to let you fall and injure yourself even more. Not on my watch."

"How far will we have to go?"

"This is going to take a few days."

"Days! You can't possibly mean to carry me for days." She reverted to Spanish. Then she let out a moan.

"Ma'am, I'm so sorry. This next one is going to hurt bad too." Clint looked over her shoulder and saw the regret on Darius's face. Lydia was hunched over and she clutched Clint's hand. Her long hair covered her face.

"Just finish it," she said in English.

Clint looked down at her bent head and at the hands holding his, and saw the wounds on her wrists. Damn, those were going to hurt as bad if not worse than the whip marks on her back. He looked around the shack and saw that each of the other men on his team had paired up with the other family members.

"How much longer Dare?" Mason asked.

"Not much, Lieutenant."

Clint had been responsible for intel on the operation. The Mexican drug cartel planned to make an example of Mr. Hidalgo today. They were bringing someone high up in the organization to the shack to watch an execution of him and his family. They were going to post it on-line as a warning to others.

Clint's team was involved because Hidalgo had been working with American DEA agents, but some of them were on the cartel's payroll. Still this wasn't enough for the Navy to be involved, but unfortunately there was a US Congressman who was implicated in the mess. So a Senator pulled some strings to ensure Hidalgo was brought to safety.

The cartel pulled the Hidalgos out of their home where they were having dinner, and brought them to the ass end of nowhere. It looked like everyone but Lydia had clothes that could weather the trek. She was in a shredded dress, shredded nylons and no shoes.

Clint ducked down and pulled out a T-Shirt from his backpack. He would've given her fatigues but the cotton material would rest more softly against her back. He found a chair and shoved it right side up and guided her to sit down now that Darius was done applying the salve on her back.

"Lydia, you're holding up the front of your dress. When Darius bandages your wrists it will fall. Let's get you into this shirt, okay?"

She looked up dazed.

"What's your name?"

Fuck.

"I'm sorry Ma'am. I'm Senior Chief Petty Officer Clint Archer. I'm a Navy SEAL. I'm part of team Midnight Delta. We're going to get you out of this hellhole."

She looked at him as she held the remains of her dress to her breasts.

"Call me Clint," he said in his most gentle voice. "I'm just going to put this over your head and pull it down, then you can put your arms through. How does that sound?"

She sighed in relief. "It sounds really good Clint."

He was careful to keep the back of the shirt from touching her wounds until the very end. He pulled out the mounds of black curls from the opening for her head. She winced when the shirt and the hair finally rested against her back, and as she struggled to get her hands through the openings for her arms.

"Let me help." He reached in and guided her limbs through, amazed at the softness of her skin. God, she was trembling so hard. She wasn't going to stay conscious for long. He looked around the shack and saw Mason giving him a hard look. They had to hurry.

Darius had gauze ready to wrap around her wrists.

"Give me your hands Lydia," Clint requested.

She squeezed tightly as Darius quickly administered to the wounds on her wrists. Quiet tears rolled down her face.

"All done, Ms. Hidalgo."

Clint let go of her hands and pulled socks out of his backpack and pulled them onto her small feet.

"Let's get you settled up on my back."

Lydia wasn't a tall woman, maybe five feet, five inches

and a little on the curvy side, in other words, a perfect armful. She wouldn't be a hardship to carry, but it was going to be tougher when she became a dead weight, and there wasn't a doubt in his mind she would be before sundown.

Clint turned and crouched down so Lydia could maneuver onto his back. She wiggled a bit so she could get a better grip, then she wrapped her arms around his neck.

"Lydia, I need you to grip my shoulders, better yet, put one arm underneath one arm and link it with the hand coming over my other shoulder. I can't have you blocking my airway."

"I'm sorry. I should have thought of that myself."

"Why? Have you ridden piggyback through the jungle before?"

"No, but it was on my bucket list," she said through gritted teeth.

Clint chuckled as he hiked her up a little bit higher, and then Darius came around front holding some rope. He heard her swift intake of breath and wished he could spare her this.

"Remember, I'm giving you my back-up knife so you can get out of this."

"Actually, I'm going to tie it so all she has to do is yank and it will give way." Clint watched Darius's swift and sure movements. He tied the cords so it was above her elbows and wouldn't slide down to her wrists.

"Ms. Hidalgo, here is the end of the rope, if you pull this, you'll be free in an instant."

"Thank you." Clint wished he could see her expression. Darius nodded.

"Okay, we need to get going." Darius swung Clint's backpack up with his, and they left the shack.

Clint tried to carry on a conversation with Lydia, anything to keep her awake, but she was too tired. When he had to climb over tree trunks she groaned in pain. Those were the worst moments, and he hated them. He looked ahead and saw the other members of the family at different levels of energy.

Finn was watching over the father, and Drake was helping the mother. Drake was second in command and the biggest member of the SEAL team. He probably should have been carrying Lydia, but everybody realized Clint made up his mind to take care of her. Therefore, Drake had Mrs. Hidalgo in case she needed to be carried next.

The younger sister, Beth, looked like she had a lot of nervous energy, and would make it for a while. Clint could tell she had been through some shit. She was paired with Mason, their Lieutenant, and he would treat her with kid gloves.

"Clint? I think I'm going to pass out. I'm sorry."

How did he tell her it would be a blessing? That the sounds of pain she was making were killing him? "Lydia, it doesn't matter."

"If I pass out, then I'm going to be harder for you to carry."

"In training I've had to carry a lot more weight than you. You're a lightweight in comparison."

"That can't be true." She shifted and held on tighter.

"SEAL training is grueling. They make sure we can handle any contingency, including carrying beautiful women through jungles." She huffed out a laugh, and warmth bathed his neck.

"So you're a sweet talker, aren't I lucky." Then she sighed, and rested her head on his shoulder and she faded into unconsciousness.

Darius, who had been taking up the rear jogged up beside him.

"I can take her for a while."

"Maybe in another mile or two."

"It's going to rain soon."

"Yeah, I was tracking a monsoon heading this way."

Drake, who had been leading, stopped at a clearing. Everyone sat down to rest.

Darius helped Clint to lay Lydia onto her side on a silver survival blanket. She didn't even stir.

"Go ask Mason how much time we're going to be here. I want to stitch up her left wrist, and start on her back." Darius was already opening up his medical gear.

Clint took one last look at Lydia and then walked towards his Lieutenant. He gave a quick chin tilt so he would walk away from the younger sister.

"I told the family they need to let us take care of Lydia," Mason said. "They want to spend time with her, and I understand. But I explained they all need to conserve their energy and our medic was the best in the Navy."

"I'm surprised they agreed."

"They're dead on their feet. They would have argued, but I think making their way across camp is too much for them." Mason looked over to where Beth was sitting against a tree. "I've been trying to get Beth to talk, but she's keeping quiet. Something bad happened. Did Lydia talk to you?"

"She said the men tried to rape her sister, but she did something to make them mad, and that's why they whipped her." Clint gritted his teeth. His T-Shirt had been soaked through with blood.

"Whatever happened to Beth wasn't good. I'm glad to hear she wasn't raped, but she's definitely been abused. She's really scared of me. Lydia's bravery is amazing, but that whipping she took is horrific."

"I wonder what the parents were doing." Mason and Clint looked over to where the older Hidalgos were huddled together. "Look, Dare wants to give Lydia some intensive first aid, can we stop for the night?"

"Yep. We'll camp here until dawn."

Clint went back to Darius and hunkered down beside him and Lydia. He was getting ready to stitch up Lydia's wrist.

"These aren't ideal circumstances."

"I didn't hear you bitching this much when you had to sew up Finn," Clint joked wanly.

"Finn couldn't give a shit about scars." Unfortunately, Clint knew the drill. He held Lydia's forearm, and waited for Darius to numb the area. Lydia didn't flinch. They waited, then Darius did a thorough cleaning of the wound before beginning to sew. He was almost done when she began to wake up.

"Please, no more," she moaned in Spanish. Clint spoke to her in a soft voice, and he felt like shit as he continued to hold her down.

"How much longer, Dare?"

"Almost done."

"Shhhh, Lydia, it's me Clint. I promise you're safe. Darius is putting stitches into your wrist so you don't get an infection. Please Lydia, listen to my voice. Can you hear me? You're safe." Clint repeated those words over and over.

Finally, she heard him. "Clint?" She stopped struggling.

"Yes Baby, it's me."

"Done."

Clint let go of Lydia. "There you go. Try to keep your wrist immobile for a while, okay? We don't want you undoing all of Darius' hard work."

Lydia tried to sit up and Clint helped her. She looked at her swollen and stitched up flesh and winced.

"Why doesn't it hurt?"

"I anesthetized the area. Even with the shot I'm going to give you, when the numbness wears off, it's going to hurt." Darius carefully measured the amount of liquid that went into the syringe and administered it.

"Will this knock her out?"

"If I give her more it will," Darius admitted.

"I don't want anymore. I refuse to weigh down Clint as he has to carry me. It's easier when I'm awake. I won't hold still for any more shots." The small woman in her baggy black shirt was staring down the two of them. She sounded like a hissing kitten. It would be comical except for the lines of pain on her face.

"Lydia, we're making camp now. I can see how much pain you're in just from your back. Let's get you something that will help you sleep through the night, okay?"

"She giving you trouble?" Finn asked as he came over with two large tarps. Lydia looked frightened and pushed closer to Clint. Finn immediately realized his mistake and crouched down in front of her.

"I'm sorry, Ma'am. I was just teasing. I love seeing you giving Darius and Clint a little bit of what for. It's good for them."

She pushed away from Clint, and he missed her warmth. She sat up straight and gave Finn a brave smile.

"It's okay. I'm just jumpy."

"I'm here to help you set up camp. Guys, hit the high ground close to the tree, it's definitely going to rain."

Clint picked up Lydia, mindful of her back. Darius and Finn spread out the ground tarp over the roots of the tree so it was up high and the rain wouldn't pool around them. Then they affixed the other tarp to the tree and some spikes in the ground so they would be covered. Lydia would be wrapped in the silver survival blanket. As far as Clint was concerned they were living large, but for a woman who had never camped in a jungle and had just been tortured, this had to be hell on Earth.

"Thank you so much," she said as she looked at what they had devised.

Both Finn and Darius gave her odd looks. Obviously their thoughts had been mirroring his own.

"It's the best we can do for you tonight, Ms. Hidalgo."

"I know, and I appreciate everything you've done for me and my family." Clint looked at her and saw nothing but sincerity. *Amazing, fucking amazing.*

"It's our job, Ma'am," Finn answered.

Darius and Finn got some foliage and put it down under the spot where Lydia was going to lay. Clint put her down on her side and covered her with a blanket. Each man was going to stick with one family member so if problems arose they would be able to protect them.

Drake had first watch, so he gave over his pack for Lydia to use as her pillow. Seconds after they got settled under the tarp it was as if the heavens opened up and started pouring buckets of water. The only saving grace was it was coming down straight instead of sideways.

Despite the rain it was hot and humid. He hadn't minded carrying Lydia. Rescuing innocents was exactly the reason he signed up to be a SEAL, but he had been getting really hot. He could have gone another couple of miles, but the other Hidalgos weren't going to make it. Mason had done the right thing to set up camp.

Even though Darius said the shot wouldn't cause Lydia to sleep, she was dozing. He looked her over and saw where the mosquitos had gotten to her arms. Now with the rain acting as a protective barrier they shouldn't be a problem, but he should have thought of bug repellant. The last thing she needed was more pain. Her eyes opened.

"I can feel you staring at me. Are you worried I'm going to be a liability?"

He snorted. "I was kicking my ass for not taking better care of you."

"What are you talking about?" She shifted and he heard the palm fronds rustle beneath the tarp.

He tugged at her hand, and brushed a spot on her upper arm. "You're getting eaten alive with bug bites."

"Clint, you can't be serious. You've carried me for miles. You have been amazing. I sure as hell haven't noticed anything as trivial as insect bites."

He guessed she hadn't. He saw where blood had seeped through the gauze at her wrists, and now he was seeing where the shirt was stuck in places from the dried blood. It was going to hurt if she moved around while she slept.

"I'll get out the repellant before we head out tomorrow. I have an MRE for you to eat right now." He pulled it out of his back pack.

"What's an MRE?"

"It stands for Meal Ready to Eat. It's not gourmet, but it beats a protein bar." He pulled out a chicken teriyaki packet and opened it for her.

"Thank you."

He tried not to wolf his down, but failed like usual. Lydia didn't seem to have much of an appetite, and only finished half of hers. He looked at her and realized her eyes were glassy.

"How are you feeling?"

"I'm fine. It hurts a little." Talk about an understatement. She had to be in a hell of a lot of pain. Clint touched her forehead. Good, no fever. But still, she needed more pain meds.

"Darius," he yelled.

"Right here. I'm your bunk mate." Darius was wearing the standard issue poncho. He squatted down next to Lydia.

"How you doing, Ms. Hidalgo?"

"Call me Lydia." She looked over her shoulder at Darius and gave him a wan attempt at a smile.

"Okay Lydia, can you tell me how you're doing? What's your pain level on a scale of one to ten?"

"Probably a four."

"Now how about you don't lie to me."

"Lying is a sin. I think I'll keep my mouth shut." She gave a wobbly smile.

"She's stubborn, she would have made a good a good SEAL." Clint was happy to see her smile even more. "Dare, she doesn't have a fever, but her eyes are glassy and she only ate half of her dinner." Clint took the food from her hand.

"Can't say I blame her; you gave her the teriyaki. You should have given her the stroganoff. Lydia, you've got to eat to keep your strength up. We brought enough to feed us and your family." Lydia turned to look at both of them, wincing in the process.

"I'll try to eat more later."

"Let's get you a shot so you can sleep."

"Okay."

It took five minutes for the shot to take effect, but when it did Clint finally relaxed. He would bet his bottom dollar her pain level had been closer to ten.

"Dare, did some of the cuts on her back need to be stitched up as well?"

"I considered it, but with all the movement, they would just get ripped out and cause more damage. It was better to do butterfly bandages."

"Dammit. What is the likelihood of infection?"

"Pretty high. Her mother told me she was sick with a cold when she was taken. We need to keep her wounds dry. We need this damn rain to stop." Lydia shifted in her sleep and moaned, then she started to cough. Darius gave her a grim look. Clint pushed closer to her front so that they were touching, trying to give her as much warmth as possible. He watched as Darius moved closer to her back without touching her, so that he too could provide some body heat.

This time Lydia let out more of a relaxed sigh. Clint closed his eyes, maybe he would be able to get some sleep.

2

───────

By day three Lydia was burning up with fever. Clint was amazed she was conscious as often as she was.

"Clint?" she whispered. "How is Beth? How are my parents?"

He looked up ahead and saw Mason was carrying Beth. They all slowed down, but by Drake's calculations they would still make the rendezvous point on time.

"They're fine, Lydia."

"I know my father has made some mistakes." She stopped and took in deep breaths. Then she started to cough. She coughed even more at night. Some of the wounds on her back were getting red and ugly, and as predicted, she was getting an infection in her lungs. Even though Darius was trying to hide it, Clint could tell he was worried.

"Don't talk Lydia, everything is going to be all right."

"Clint, you have to promise me..." She coughed again.

"I'll promise you anything, just stop talking."

"Beth. You have to promise you'll look after Beth. My father might be in trouble when we reach America, but my mother will stand by him no matter what, she always does. Beth will be all alone." She coughed and her wet hair spilled over his shoulder. "Please take care of Beth."

"I will Lydia. I'll take care of both of you. You have my word."

She coughed again. She couldn't seem to stop, her chest rattled, and then she passed out.

"Darius," he yelled.

"Halt!" Mason called out.

Clint was half aware of the rest of the family as they just about fell down where they stopped. All of the Hidalgos were on their last legs. Mason knew Lydia was in trouble, and was making the decision to take a break so Darius could attend to her.

Clint found the best coverage he could under a large tree, and wasn't surprised when Finn and Drake had tarps out to protect Lydia. Darius had his back pack out with all of his medical supplies.

Clint sank down at Lydia's feet and pulled off her wet socks, and dried her off as best he could before sliding his last pair of socks on her feet. He didn't look up to see what his friend was doing. He didn't want to see the look in his eyes. Mason came over to see what was going on.

"Mason, we need to camp here for the night," Darius said grimly.

"We can't."

"Then we have to have two hours."

"Dare, there's only four hours of daylight left. We need all of it if we want to make it to the rendezvous in two days." Mason set his hand on Clint's shoulder. "You're damn near played out. Let Drake take her for the rest of the day. It'll help speed things along."

"That's bullshit. You know it's the parents slowing us down."

"Right now they are but in another hour it'll be you."

Clint looked up in his Lieutenant's eyes and realized he was right. "Okay."

Lydia groaned. Darius had stripped Lydia down to her upper buttocks and had three syringes in his hand. He was injecting her in her hip. "I need everyone's clean shirts now. We need to keep her warm, and the wounds on her back dry. The rain is dripping down inside the poncho."

Seeing the bloody and infected areas on her caramel colored skin made Clint sick. He really thought the antibiotics and antiseptic ointment would have helped her.

"Why isn't she getting better with the medicine?"

"It's the Goddamn rain," Darius said bitterly. "It keeps washing away the antiseptic and it's dripping into her mouth and nose and she's damn close to pneumonia if she doesn't already have it."

"How can that be? It's got to be eighty degrees," Finn asked.

"She was ripe for infection. She was already sick when they took her, remember?"

"Okay, so the shots you just gave her will take care of things, right?" Clint insisted. There was no other answer but 'yes'.

Darius just looked at him.

"Don't you tell me 'no'. That's not acceptable." Clint turned to Drake. "I'll carry her. You're the biggest, you pick up whichever family member is slowing our asses down. We *are* making it to the chopper and Lydia is going to be just fine."

"Chief, that's not your call to make," Mason growled.

"Wrong. I'm making it my call. I promised Lydia I would take care of her. I'm not letting her down when she needs me the most."

Mason stared at him, water dripping off the edge of his poncho, it seemed like the longest moment of Clint's life.

"Okay. But the minute you're holding us back Drake's taking her."

"I wouldn't have it any other way, Sir."

Clint helped Darius bundle Lydia back up. Then they carefully put her up on his back. She didn't make a sound. He couldn't decide if he was happy about that or not. He'd never felt such terror in his life.

The last four hours of the march we're grueling. They reminded him of his BUD/S training. As he did during his training, he just persevered. One step in front of the other, but this time the goal was so much more important.

He didn't hear when Mason called a halt. Drake had to get in front of him to get his attention.

"Thanks man."

"Not a problem. Finn's already started setting up a place for the two of you."

Clint hadn't noticed them stopping because he had been concentrating on walking and listening to Lydia's breathing. He thought it was a little bit better and not so congested. He wished Darius had a stethoscope in his backpack.

He appreciated that the spot was already laid out with leaves and other foliage to make her comfortable. He watched as the tarp was laid out on top of it. Darius was kneeling beside it, his face blank.

Drake helped Clint lower Lydia into a seating position.

He and Darius pulled off the layers of shirts, then laid her on her stomach. The wounds looked even more inflamed.

"Dare, what's going wrong. I thought they would improve. You put on the ointment, they stayed dry."

"These conditions are the worst possible for her wounds. She needs a hospital."

"But her breathing has improved. She isn't coughing, and her chest isn't rattling." Darius turned her over on her side, and put his ear up to her sternum. Clint winced, he hated to see Lydia's modesty impinged on like that, even though he knew his friend was being clinical. Clint looked up, all of the other men had turned away.

"Let's get her dressed again," Darius said.

"So she's better, right?"

Darius didn't look at him, and then he knew. His shoulders sagged.

"Just tell me."

"The congestion has gotten so bad, that it's not moving. We've got to push more fluids into her."

"I try to get her to drink, but she's unconscious, and when I wake her up, it just dribbles out of her mouth."

"You've got to try harder, Clint. It's a matter of life and death. She's at a high risk of dehydration. But be careful she doesn't choke." Darius was shaking her and putting the canteen up to her lips. "The good news is that you carrying her has been a good thing. Keeping her upright and jostling her around has helped to keep things moving in her chest. Tonight she needs to rest upright." That didn't sound very comfortable.

"If moving her around is such a good thing, why is she doing so poorly?"

"It's the infection in her back, it has moved quickly to her lungs, and the rain and humidity has done a number on her. I'm going to administer the highest dose of antibiotics I can."

"You mean you haven't before?"

Darius just looked at him, and Clint realized he had. Fuck. They just had to get to the rendezvous point as fast as possible. She needed a hospital. Failure was not an option.

That night Lydia had her first nightmare.

"Get away from my sister," she rasped in Spanish. "Take me." She started to cry. Dry wrenching sobs. She hit him and groaned as her fists connected to his chest, injuring her wrists.

"Wake her up. Get her to drink some water." Clint glowered over her head at Darius.

"Lydia, you're safe." She shook her head wildly.

"I'll do anything. Anything you want, just don't hurt my sister. I can make you feel so good." She talked softly he could barely make out her words, her voice was ruined from her illness.

Her hands changed to claws, belying her words. Clint ducked, not wanting to manhandle her.

"Baby, can you hear me. It's me Clint. You have to wake up."

"Watch me strip for you." She tried for his face again with her nails, and then Darius reached from behind and as gently as he could and grasped her forearms.

"No..." she wailed. She coughed and coughed and coughed. Until it turned into one gasping wheeze. She struggled so hard often times pushing her injured back against Darius' chest and both men did what they could to position her so it wouldn't happen. All the time, Clint spoke to her in Spanish, urgently trying to get her to come back to the present.

"Dare, please give her something for the pain. Give her something to go to sleep."

"You'll have to hold her down, I need her to be still."

Clint's breath hitched. He forced his fists to unclench so he could cup her face in his hands, resting his forehead against hers. "Lydia, baby, it's me Clint. You're safe. The men who hurt you are dead. You're having a nightmare. You're sick and you need to wake up." Over and over he whispered in Spanish. Finally, he thought to start speaking in English, and that was what seemed to do the trick.

"Clint?" It was a mere whisper. She turned her head and coughed.

"It's me." Darius held up the canteen. "You need to drink some water."

"Not thirsty."

"Doesn't matter. You have to drink." He brought the canteen to her lips, and she took a couple of sips. "More, you have to drink more." She did.

Darius prepped a syringe.

"Dare is going to give you a shot."

"Okay." That she acquiesced so easily told them both how bad her pain was. Darius administered it. She hissed out a sigh.

"Good girl."

"I'm cold, but I'm hot too."

"It's the fever," Darius said. "I'm going to go snag another survival blanket from one of the guys."

"Don't go out into the rain. It's too much of a bother." They both looked at one another over her head. Darius left the makeshift tent. Clint gathered her closer, careful not to touch her back. It was amazing how much heat was coming off her body. Her beautiful brown eyes were so glassy, it scared him to death.

He could feel the heat radiating from her body.

She started to cough.

"Oh good." Darius ducked his head under the tarp. "Coughing is good. It's when you're not coughing that I worry. Lydia, you're going to need to sleep sitting up tonight." He put the extra blanket on top of her, and they both helped her into a sitting position against Clint's backpack.

The coughing seemed to have worn her out. She opened her mouth to say something and then she was asleep.

"Is that normal?" Clint asked.

"She's really sick. I'm surprised how well she's doing."

"This is doing well?" Clint asked incredulously.

"Yes. We'll see how she is in the morning. Hopefully the antibiotics help. I'm encouraged she spoke coherently tonight. She might..."

Clint didn't ask any more questions. It was clear where Darius was going with that, and he just didn't want to face it. He laid his head next to Lydia, and went into the light combat sleep that allowed him to listen to her breathing as he rested. He was damned if she would drift away on his watch.

"CLINT, you need to rest. You're stumbling." He barely heard her, and it wasn't because of the rain which was finally letting up. It was because her voice was little more than a whisper.

"I'm fine. I'm a SEAL. This is what we do."

"Even in Mexico, we've heard of Navy SEALs. You eat nails for breakfast, and have a beautiful girl in every city." Her weak laughter tickled his ear.

She was awake because he just made her drink some water. No matter how much he coaxed she refused part of a protein bar, finally she told him she would just throw it up. Since she gagged drinking the water he had to agree with her assessment.

"Marines are the ones with beautiful girls in every city. SEALs are more discerning; we want the right girl."

Again, she laughed. "I might not have brothers, but I went to school with enough boys to know that's not true."

He felt her head fall against the crook of his neck, a sign she would soon be asleep.

"Lydia, maybe not every SEAL is looking for the right girl, but I know I am. I'm looking for a brave girl, a girl who believes in family, and a girl who has honor."

"She sounds nice. I hope you find her." Lydia's voice trailed off into sleep.

It looked like the whip marks were festering even worse than they had that morning, and Lydia wouldn't wake up.

"Dare, do something," it was a hoarse plea.

"We're almost to help." Dare didn't meet his eyes.

They'd taken a break. Clint took one last look at Lydia then he staggered over to where Mason was standing. He motioned him away from Beth.

"Mason, can't we get going?"

"I radioed the chopper. They'll be at the extraction point at the designated time. We're going to be early if we leave now, so we have time for this break. Mr. and Mrs. Hidalgo need it. Let Lydia rest."

"Mason, we have to get her to a hospital."

"Don't you think I know that," Mason growled. Then he took a deep breath and put his hand on Clint's shoulder. "I'm sorry man. I'm worried too. We'll get her there. She's in the best hands possible with Dare. Go back to her, I'll make sure we get to the chopper on time."

"I know, Mase." Clint went back to Lydia.

He sat down and carefully pulled her against him. He spoke to her in Spanish, then remembered how she had responded better to English during her nightmare and switched languages. Her eyelids fluttered.

"We're going to be in the States soon. We'll get you to a hospital. Your family will be safe just like we promised." He could swear her expression relaxed and he took an easier breath. He pushed her matted hair away from her face.

"Just hang on Baby, please. I'm begging you, hang on."

Clint rocked her gently until it was time to load up. Darius helped to place her on his back, ensuring she was secure and safe.

Once again, Darius took up the rear and they headed off towards their final destination point.

SOMETHING WAS WRONG. Really wrong.

"Dare!" Clint screamed as the chopper whirled overhead. His friend helped to lower Lydia onto the ground. Clint frantically felt for Lydia's pulse at the base of her neck.

Darius shoved him out of the way and started to

perform CPR. The huey settled into the clearing as Mason ran over to Clint.

"Mase, I didn't feel her pulse."

Mason signaled to the corpsman who brought a stretcher and an oxygen mask. They whisked Lydia into the belly of the bird continuing to perform CPR, with Darius running behind them. Mason directed the rest of the civilians to follow. Finn and Drake were next, and then he pulled in Clint.

Clint skidded on his knees to the pallet holding Lydia. They had an IV in her arm. The corpsman working on her stopped compressing her chest. At long fucking last the corpsman gave Clint a thumbs-up. He moved away and Clint saw her breathe on her own. He touched his forehead to hers.

"Thank God. Thank God."

THERE WAS a knock on the door.

"Come in."

"Hello, Beautiful," he said in a low voice.

Lydia looked up from her hospital bed and did a double take, or was it a triple take? She recognized the voice, but not the man. There was no mistaking the rumble that was Clint Archer's voice, but this clean shaven, sandy haired man in a button down white shirt and black jeans was somebody new.

"Lydia?" This time he didn't sound quite as confident. That was when she noticed the flower arrangement in his hands.

"You brought me flowers? Roses?" Nobody had brought her flowers since she had been in the hospital.

She had to blink fast so no tears fell. "Clint, how did you find me? They put me under an assumed name." Lydia cleared her throat to get the words out.

He walked partway into the room and smiled at her.

"It took a while to find out where they put you. Then it took a little bit more time to arrange leave so I could be here with you."

She pulled the thin blanket up a little higher to cover the cotton gown the hospital provided.

What was he doing here? She was much better and going to be released by the end of the week, so why was she having a tough time breathing?

"I wanted to call, but like I said, it took a while before I could find you. Luckily, after I did, I found out you were still going to be here by the time I could get leave. So I figured I would just show up. That's all right, isn't it?" He sounded unsure, having watched as she pulled up the blanket.

"Of course." His eyes narrowed as she pulled the blanket even higher.

"It doesn't look like it. It looks like I'm making you uncomfortable."

"You are," she blurted out.

He ran his hand through his hair; his other still holding the vase of flowers. "Damn Lydia, I never meant to do that. I just hated the way they took you away. I got them to tell me you were going to be okay, and that you were going to make a full recovery. But the US Marshalls took you into their system and refused to let me know how to find you. Making you feel bad or upset you is the last thing I wanted to do."

"Oh Clint, that came out wrong. I dreamed of seeing you again. Only I wanted to see you one day when I was normal. Not sick. Not in a hospital bed. I wanted you to see me like I really am. I'm strong." *But she wasn't strong, she was babbling.*

"Are you kidding? You're one of the strongest people I know."

She snorted. "Yeah sure. You always have to carry strong people through a jungle." She started to tear up.

"Hey, Lydia, what's wrong?" He was across the room and beside her bed faster than she could blink.

"It's this damned pneumonia. My emotions are all over the place. Then having you here. I'm so happy, but I just wanted..."

"It's okay. I think I understand." He set the flowers on the nightstand.

"Well then, you're doing better than me."

He chuckled and reached his hand out towards her face. She caught it and brought it to her cheek. He felt so warm, so alive. She kissed his palm.

"Thank you for coming, Clint."

She stared into the beautiful hazel eyes of the man who had literally saved her life. He finally cleared his throat.

"How is Beth?"

"She puts on a brave front when she comes to visit, but I'm really worried about her. I'll be happy when I'm out of here and we can be together."

"Always trying to take care of everyone aren't you?"

"No I'm not." Clint laughed. He looked so much younger than when he had been in the jungle. Lydia yawned.

"I can come back later if you need to get some rest."

"If I hear one more person tell me I need rest and take it easy, I might have to kill them."

Clint threw back his head and laughed. Her breath stopped. Literally stopped. In all the time she had known him in the jungle, she never heard him laugh like that. She wanted to hear it again.

"What?"

"Huh?"

"You're staring at me, Lydia. Are you okay?"

"I just never heard you laugh like that." He picked up one of her hands, brought it to his cheek, and then kissed her palm.

"Baby, there was never a moment I felt like laughing. I was scared almost every minute."

"You saved me. How could you be scared?"

"Lydia, you were so sick. You almost died. I was scared every minute." She stroked his cheek.

"Well you don't have to worry now. I'm much better. The pneumonia has pretty much cleared up."

"Yep, that's what the hospital records said."

"You hacked the hospital records?"

"Only at a very high level. I wanted to see what your prognosis was, and if you were getting the right level of care. Your doctors are very highly regarded."

"You hacked my doctors?"

"Yep." He didn't even have the grace to look guilty. He was still standing there holding her hand.

"Wait, how do you know how to hack so many things?"

"It's kind of what I do. Everyone on the team has a specialty. Mine is computers." Lydia couldn't help the grin that spread over her face.

"What?"

"Nothing."

"Bullshit. That's a pretty big smile for nothing. Spill it, lady."

"Let me adjust the bed so I'm sitting up." Looking at her, he immediately let go of her hand, and put his arm around her so he was supporting her. Then he found the remote that brought the bed up to the proper height so she could sit up.

"Is this better?" His arm was now trapped between her back and her pillows. She looked up at him from beneath her lowered lashes.

"It's much better." She couldn't begin to explain what the feel of him was doing to her insides. It made her happy to see Clint looking flushed as he withdrew his arm.

"So what makes you so interested in my hacking abilities?"

"I would love to know some of your techniques. I have studied up on you brash upstarts, and I actually wrote a paper on a hacker who broke into a Fortune 100's e-mail server and had all e-mails blind cc everyone in the company for a day. It was amazing how much confidential information was leaked in the hour before the server was shut down. It was done by a fourteen-year-old in Nebraska."

"Yep, Shelly Reynolds. She's really gifted."

"The only thing I couldn't find out was her punishment. I checked all my sources, but this was one of the few times I came up empty. It really pissed me off. I could never find out whether they prosecuted her as a juvenile or an adult, or what happened."

"I bet you couldn't." Clint grinned over his shoulder as he pulled up a chair.

"Do you know? You can't. I asked every contact I had. I have a lot of friends in law enforcement and computer science, and some who might have broken some hacking laws themselves. So it's really weird they couldn't find out what happened to Shelly."

"That's an odd assortment of friends. How'd you manage to get them?" Clint sat down with his foot resting on his knee.

"You tell me what you know first. *And,* how you know it."

"I know it because I'm military. What I know is Shelly was recruited by Uncle Sam, and she'll be enlisting on her eighteenth birthday."

"It's not against her will is it?" Lydia leaned against the bedrail so she could get closer to Clint and see his expression even more clearly.

"No the draft ended years ago. Like I said, she was recruited and she's pretty excited. She is going to be able to play with the biggest and best toys, and some of the brightest minds. She'll never be bored again."

"How exciting for her."

"You mean that, don't you?" Clint gave her an odd look. "So tell me how you got such an interesting group of friends in the US."

"Not just the US, but all across the world. I have a double major, Criminology and Computer Science. I did a lot of social networking. I'm almost finished with my-" Lydia bit her lip and looked down at the white blanket covering her.

"What Lydia? What are you almost finished with?"

"Never mind, it doesn't matter." She didn't want to talk about it. She gave him a big smile. "Clint, I'm so happy you came and found me."

"Talk to me Lydia, don't hide from me. We've been through too much to start hiding now." His chair scraped as he dragged it across the floor so he was now sitting right next to her and he held out his hand. She clasped it.

"You're right. It's not that it's a big secret. Anyway, I'm surprised you haven't run a check on me."

"I thought about it, but I wanted to get to know you the old fashioned way." She could see he was telling the truth.

"I appreciate that. It seemed like there were a lot of things ripped out of my hands when we first met. I appreciate you not violating my privacy—except for the hospital records of course." She hoped her grin took the sting out of her words. It must have, because he grinned back.

"So now will you tell me?"

"I was working on my Masters of Computer Science."

"Pretty impressive. What were you planning on doing with that?"

"With my education in Criminology I intended to work for the Federal Ministerial Police." She watched him carefully. It was her experience that men were not happy about her career aspirations. She'd only had two boyfriends before, and in both cases they thought she should do something a little more feminine. Preferably, along the lines of becoming a housewife.

Stupid girl, you're looking at a Navy SEAL and thinking he's going to be okay with you wanting to work in law enforcement? Dream on!

"Being a police officer is a noble profession, but isn't it pretty difficult in Mexico City?" She couldn't get a read on him. He seemed sincere, but she heard a 'but'. She waited. "What type of career were you hoping to have?" His thumb caressed the top of her hand.

"I spoke to some of my professors at the University.

There is definitely a need in the cyber-crimes unit. They're also trying to get more women in higher ranks within the police force."

His hand tightened on hers.

"What?"

He let out a long breath. "Haven't a lot of the higher ranking officers been targeted by the cartels and gangs?"

"The police can't let fear stop them from doing their job. Anyway, it would be years before I would be promoted. I would first have to prove myself."

"Jesus, Lydia." He looked at her and she couldn't drag her eyes away from his, this time it was her turn to question him.

"What?"

"You amaze me. It wasn't just circumstances in the jungle. You're just as noble and brave in your normal life as you were when you saved your sister." She snatched her hand back.

"I'm nothing. I just do what needs to be done."

"Lydia, you know that's not true. You're special." He took her hand back and clasped it between both of his. He was so warm and it felt good. She shook her head.

"How about saying you're a tiny bit above the norm?" he teased.

"Well I *am* pretty good with computers."

He laughed and she joined him.

"But seriously Clint, we don't know what I'm like. You're the one who's been tested. I am still just taking classes. You're the one who's serving his country."

"Okay, so now I know you can't take a compliment. Let's table this conversation for a while and talk about something we can agree on. What have you been doing for fun in this place?"

Lydia looked guiltily over at the drawer in the table next to her bed.

"Toys? I always like finding toys in a woman's nightstand." He reached for the drawer and opened it up. "Score!" He reached in and pulled out her computer, headset and game controller. "What do you play?"

"Lots of things." *God this was embarrassing.*

"Please say *League of Legends*." He couldn't actually like the same online game that she liked, it wasn't possible, not in a million years.

"You're messing with me. If you play, you play *Counter-Strike*."

"Honey, I live *Counter-Strike*. Nexus all the way."

"Oh my God, you're serious. You actually play. *League of Legends*? Clint this is amazing!"

Lydia's heart sped up and a wide smile spread over her face. "Tomorrow I'm bringing my computer when I visit and I'm going to kick your ass."

"You're going to be here tomorrow?"

"Didn't you hear me? I took some leave. I'll be here for the next four days. You're stuck with me until they whisk you away into hiding." Her grin got even wider.

For the next hour they discussed game strategy, and she realized inside the armor of a SEAL beat the heart of a fellow nerd.

3

"BEAUTIFUL, WE HAVE TO QUIT MEETING LIKE THIS."

Lydia looked up in shock. Clint couldn't be here. After leaving the hospital the first time, the US Marshalls gave her a new last name, and she resigned herself to never seeing him again.

"Clint! How did you know?" She started to cough so hard, her chest rattled.

"Fuck Lydia, do I need to get the nurse?" He rushed over to her. He saw her reaching for the glass by her bed and helped her position the straw to her mouth. She drank and the coughing finally subsided.

He pushed her damp hair off of her forehead. His eyes looked so soft and worried she had to force herself not to cry. Dammit, she hated this illness. Her emotions were all over the board.

He put the glass down, gathered her up, and tucked her face into the crook of his neck.

"Let it out, Baby, I'm not going to think less of you if you cry. It's going to be all right."

"I'm not going to fucking cry. There's no crying in football or soccer, or whatever you call it."

"Baseball."

"Fine. Baseball." Lydia bit her lip so hard she could taste blood. "*Dios*, it's never going to be all right ever again." And it wouldn't.

"Tell me. How the fuck did you end up back in the hospital? On one hand, I'm so damn mad you let yourself get run down again." Despite the tone of his words he pushed her gently away so he could look her in the eye.

"On the other hand, I'm so fucking thankful you got sick again so I could find you." He kissed her forehead. "Now tell me how you got sick."

"Mama got ill. It was just the flu. Papa got so worried she was going to die he said the stress of being in hiding was killing his family so he wasn't going to testify. When I ended up getting ill too, I knew I couldn't let on."

His eyes glinted fire.

"You could have died! Pneumonia is serious shit. Jesus Lydia, I could just shake you." He kissed the top of her head.

"Papa would have had more second thoughts. He has to testify. Those agents have to testify against Guzman."

"So if you didn't tell them you were sick how did they find out?"

She burrowed closer to Clint wanting to sink into his warmth. She didn't want to answer him, because she knew how mad he would be. He let her get away with it for long minutes. He seemed to need the connection as well.

Finally. "Answer me, Lydia."

"Apparently I didn't wake up. They had to call an ambulance."

"You're so getting a spanking when you get better." She

laughed, and then it turned into a cough. He held her up while helping her drink some more water. Then he adjusted the bed into an upright position.

"How long are you here for?" she asked.

"Nobody knows I'm here. This is one of those 'ask for forgiveness' kind of things."

"What?"

"You know the old saying, 'It is better to ask for forgiveness than permission'. If I asked for permission, they might have said 'No.' Not my lieutenant. Mason would have said 'yes'. But our captain might have said 'no'."

"Oh God. Are you going to be in trouble?"

He didn't meet her eyes.

"Clint, you've got to go back."

"Nope. I left a message for Mason. He knows where to find me if he needs me. I can be back in San Diego in four hours if I have to. Right now, I'm where I need to be."

More tears leaked. "I can't seem to stop crying."

"It's okay, Baby. I couldn't stop swearing when the computer pinged and you were back in the hospital." He lowered the bedrail and sat down next to her hip.

"How did you find me? They didn't even use the same alias as the last time."

"I have certain parameters set up. There have been a couple of false reads, but when a beautiful girl with pneumonia in the DFW area showed up in the hospital, I checked her out. I had a gut feeling, don't ask me how, but I knew it was you. God dammit, they had you in ICU! Do you know how fucking serious that was?" His face was so close to hers she could smell the toothpaste he used.

"But Papa-"

"I don't give a shit. Lydia, you're more important than him."

"But I'm not more important than putting those animals away."

"Yes. You. Are." He was serious. He sat up and raked both hands through his short sandy hair.

"Clint, we haven't seen or talked to one another in over a month. I'm going to go into the Witness Protection Program. You can't allow me to mean that much to you."

"Really? Are you saying I don't mean that much to *you*?"

There was a buzzing sound. He pulled out his phone and winced and answered it.

"Yeah Mason, I'm here in Dallas." He paused. "Yeah, I'm with Lydia." He paused again. "Yep, you got it in one. It's not good, but she's got good doctors, and she's going to get better. She doesn't seem to have the sense God gave an ant." He gave her a hard stare. She gulped. He listened for long minutes. "I appreciate the choice, Mason. Thank you." He sighed. "So I wouldn't have to be there until tomorrow night?"

Lydia couldn't believe how much it mattered to her. It shouldn't matter. Nothing would ever come of their time together.

"Yeah, now I've seen her for myself I can breathe again. I'll take a flight back to San Diego tomorrow afternoon. Thanks man. I'll be there for the team." He pressed end on the phone and dropped it back into the side pocket of his cargo pants.

"You should go back today."

"I'm staying Lydia."

He cupped her cheek and stared down at her. She finally looked away, embarrassed by his scrutiny.

"Baby, please don't scare me like this again."

"I won't. I promise."

The lines in his forehead eased. He smiled. "I didn't bring my computer; I knew you were too sick to play video games. Hell, look at you, you can barely keep your eyes open. Just sleep beautiful."

He was right, all of the conversation had worn her out. But she didn't want to sleep when he was actually there with her. He was going to have to leave on some secret mission, and then she would be going into hiding again.

He must have seen the angst on her face. His other hand came up and cupped her other cheek, his thumb tracing her dry bottom lip.

"Rest baby. I'll be here when you wake up. I promise."

"Clint!" Lydia looked around the darkened room, and then saw him sitting with his e-reader.

"I'm right here, baby." He got up immediately and came to her. He grabbed her hand and brushed back her hair. "Damn, you still feel feverish."

"I'm feeling better. It must be the *rest*." She gave him a grin.

"I'm glad one of us can smile about this."

"How soon before you have to leave?"

"I have another hour."

"Were you going to leave without saying good-bye?" She felt the damn tears welling. God dammit, when was she going to stop being so weepy and needy?

"Absolutely not. Lydia, I promised I would be here when you woke up. I keep my promises. So even if I had to wake you up before leaving, that's what I was going to do."

He squatted down beside the bed so they were eye level. "You believe me, don't you?"

"Yes. Your word is golden."

"Okay, no more tears. They kill me." She looked at him, and realized he was telling the truth. Her pain was his pain. Oh God, she couldn't let him feel this way. This was the last time they were ever going to see one another, maybe she could make him hate her.

"So what do you want to talk about, the fact this is going to be the last time we're ever going to see one another?" She bit her lip and tried not to gasp for air. This time she couldn't stop the tears from falling. Clint looked as anguished as she felt.

"Lydia-"

"I need you to get the hell out of here. Now."

"Wait a minute." He was frowning at her.

"I mean it Archer." If there was any food in her body, she would throw up. As it was she had to force herself not to gag. "I'm going into the witness protection program. My father is a criminal."

"Your father isn't a criminal. He made some bad mistakes which he's correcting."

"You don't know everything."

"I don't give a shit."

"Get out of here. I appreciate the visits. You've been a great guy. I can't thank you enough for having saved me. For having saved my family. But that's all it was. That's all it can be. I've been living in a dream, building little happy endings."

"Exactly, there's more here, you mean more to me than-"

"Shut up and leave."

"No. You mean so much to-"

"Well nothing can come of this. I'm sick. My life is in ruins. I don't need one more thing to feel bad about. I'm begging you. Leave."

"Oh Baby, this isn't going to work you know. I'm not going to leave here being mad at you. I care too much." He stood and bent over the bedrail, his hands framed her face. He stared deep into her eyes.

"You're one of the best things that has ever happened to me Lydia Hidalgo."

"Ahhh, Clint." What could she say to that? To him?

"You need to leave now." He looked at his watch. "I'll never forget you Clint."

"There is no way this is over, Baby."

"Yes it is. You need to forget me like I need to forget you."

He came around to the other side of the bed, furthest from the door. He pushed down the bedrail and eased his hands under her back and legs.

"What are you doing?"

He lifted her, got into the bed, and arranged it so she was lying, over him. *Oh God, it felt so good.*

"In the little time we have left tell me the truth." She looked into his eyes and found she couldn't lie anymore.

"I don't want you to disappear again."

He cradled her head under his chin, and his hand rested against her forehead. He kissed her hair.

"Tell me about your nightmares. Tell me about your dreams. I want to know everything there is about Lydia Hidalgo."

"Clint, this is so wrong. Nothing can come of it."

"Give me this. Give me this time. This is my dream."

"I'll give you this if you'll then give me my dream."

"Anything."

"First, you tell me everything there is about Clint Archer, then you promise to forget me." He clutched her close, she felt his warm breath on her neck.

"Ahhh, Lydia. You hold your dreams close, and I'll hold my dreams close."

4

LYDIA WOKE UP IN A COLD SWEAT. HER FATHER AND MOTHER were standing over her bed, her mother had tears tracing down her face, and her father looked anguished.

"Where am I?"

"You're in the hospital again," her mom whispered. Everything hurt. Lydia felt like she was under water. Even asking the one question had taken an enormous amount of energy.

"Why?"

Her mother's eyes darted over to her father, and Lydia remembered. She remembered being strong once. This wasn't her.

"I relapsed didn't I?"

"It's all my fault." Now tears dripped down her father's face.

She couldn't deny it, so she didn't say anything.

He turned away from Lydia's hospital bed, her mother tried to grab him, but he fled the room.

Lydia struggled to lift herself up, but fell back on the bed.

"You must rest daughter."

Lydia watched her mother twist the straps of her purse.

"I'm so sorry. I should have made him stop. I was pretty sure what he was doing. I should have stopped him, but I wanted a better life for you and Beth."

Lydia's tears started in earnest. She had always suspected that her mother knew about her father's illegal activities, but to have it confirmed devastated her.

"Where is Beth?" It took all of Lydia's concentration to ask the question, she was dizzy and it hurt to talk. The pneumonia had sapped all of her strength. She hated the toll this illness took on her body. It seemed like this third bout was the worst.

"She has to be close by, you know our keepers won't let her get far."

Lydia grimaced. She realized her mother was bitter. They had been cooped up in the safe house now for four months. But they were safe. And, hadn't *both* of her parents brought it on themselves?

"How long," Lydia started to cough.

"Sweetheart, you need to stop talking. You need your rest."

"Mama," Lydia said between bouts of coughing.

The door to her room opened. A woman came in, and it took Lydia a moment to recognize Dr. Woods. God she hated this, even her memory was hazy when she got so sick.

"How are you doing, Lydia?"

"I–" Lydia started to cough. The doctor came over and put the stethoscope to her chest and listened.

"You're breathing is better than it was yesterday."

"How long will I need to be here?" Lydia pressed her

hand against her chest, trying to stop the wheezing.

"You were here two weeks last time and you still ended up back here. I think it's safe to say you'll have to be here longer this time."

"How much longer?"

"We'll have to wait and see. Lydia, you've already been here for five days," Dr. Woods said as she took her pulse. "We're putting you on even stronger medications this time. We'll monitor you closely."

Lydia fought back tears. For a moment she wondered why she was crying, then she remembered it was just another side effect of her illness. She saw her mother and doctor looking at her with sympathy. She hated it. She hated everything. She clenched her fists.

"You *will* get better," Dr. Woods assured her.

"Until the next time I end up here, right? Isn't my immune system pretty much shot?"

"Why would you think that?"

"I just assumed that since I'm here for a third time I must just be prone to this now." She wiped the tears from her face, causing her arm to ache.

"Lydia, it's amazing you made it out of the jungle alive. I don't know if you remember, but I was one of the doctors that treated you. The injuries you received from the whipping and the infection because it was unlike anything we'd seen here in Dallas. Your recovery was nothing short of a miracle."

Everything Dr. Woods described was a blur. The only thing Lydia remembered during that time was Clint. She remembered the fierce look in his eyes when he demanded she stay alive. His hazel eyes were burned into her memory, along with a voice that sounded like a truck driving on a gravel road. It would rumble and growl and somehow make her feel protected and safe. And now she would never see him again, at least she prayed she wouldn't, because it would hurt too much. She started to cry in earnest.

"Lydia, my God, what's wrong sweetheart?" Her mother looked frantic.

"I'm going to get you something to rest."

"No! I only just woke up." But then the idea of oblivion began to sound good.

"Actually this is the third time you've woken up, you're just disoriented. You've been restless and in pain. You need real rest this time. Your body needs sleep, Lydia." The doctor pressed the call button and a nurse let herself into the room. She looked at the doctor who nodded, and the nurse injected something into Lydia's IV.

"You'll sleep through the night, and then we can discuss your recovery in the morning."

CLINT SLAMMED the door on his rental car and made a run for the hospital entrance. The rain was really coming down, making him grimace. He used to like the rain but not anymore. It reminded him too much of the torrential downpour he had carried Lydia through in the Mexican jungle. God he still had nightmares of her groans and whimpers, and then there was that moment when he thought she was dead. Even now the thought could damn near take him to his knees.

He spotted Beth Hidalgo as soon as he entered the lobby of the hospital. She was as lovely as her sister, with waves of dark hair and big black eyes. He grabbed her up into a hug, and she went stiff as a board.

"Ah Beth, I'm sorry, I forgot."

"It's alright, Clint. You'd think I'd be over it by now." Clint released her slowly, and kissed the top of her head. *Those fucking animals.* He and his team should have killed them more slowly.

"It takes time," he assured her. He watched as her chin trembled and she forced herself to hold his gaze.

"But nothing really happened. Lydia sacrificed herself for me, and then...and then." Tears filled her eyes.

"Are you still seeing a counselor?" Beth frowned.

"Yes." She gave him a clipped answer and then turned away from him. "Let's go upstairs. Mama and Papa just left." Clint followed the young woman into the elevator. He called and told her he was coming. He was going to need some backup this time.

He nodded to the man who had been leaning unobtrusively against a wall, watching the two of them. He recognized him from his previous visit. He was the US Marshall who shadowed Beth.

The three of them waited for the elevator, and Clint realized how much he hated this hospital. He was sick of visiting Lydia in hospitals. He really wanted her to be well. He wanted both of the Hidalgo women to be well. Then he re-thought his position, if Lydia weren't in the hospital, he wouldn't have found her, however he had been *damn close* to finding her. Thank God the Marshall's put up with his presence when she was in the hospital.

When they got off on the fifth floor it was easy to determine which room was hers. There was another US Marshall outside her door. He didn't recognize him. Beth introduced Clint to Ed, and he provided his military ID to the man.

"The doctor just left. She said that Lydia was probably

going to sleep through until morning," the big man explained.

"Thanks, Ed," Beth said. "If she's asleep, we'll leave."

Clint opened the door and held it for Beth to go through. His gaze immediately zeroed in on Lydia. Damn, she looked so frail in the hospital bed. He had just seen her two months ago as she was discharged from this same hospital and she had been looking so happy and healthy. To see her like this about broke his heart.

"Beth?" Lydia didn't open her eyes.

"I'm here and I brought a friend."

Lydia turned her head on the pillow and slowly lifted her lids. It seemed to take a moment for her to focus.

"You came. Oh Clint, you came." Her smile lit up the hospital room, and filled every fiber of his being. He was at her bedside in an instant and gripping her outstretched hand.

"I'll always come for your baby. Always." Her face might be thin and ravaged by illness but she was the most beautiful woman on the planet.

Lydia's smile dimmed. "You need to leave. Nothing's changed."

She was right, but it still hurt to hear her say it.

"I'm staying. I don't care what's going to happen in the future, for right now you need me, and I *need* to be with *you*." Despite her verbal rejection her grip never lessened. He brought her hand to his lips and kissed her palm. He heard the door open and close. Bless Beth, she knew they needed this time alone.

"Clint, you know we can never have a future together. I'm either going into Witness Protection, or if Papa decides not to testify, I'll be going back to Mexico. Don't do this to yourself. Please don't. I don't want you hurt. Anyway, you only know me as someone who is a patient in a hospital, or someone who needs to be rescued. Just leave, it's for the best."

"That's bullshit and you know it. I know you, Lydia Hidalgo, and over my dead body will you be going back to Mexico."

"But if my father..." her voice began to slur with the drugs they gave her.

"I hope so..." Lydia's eyes closed and she drifted off to sleep. Clint looked around the room and pulled up a chair. He would watch over her as she slept. He couldn't bear the thought of leaving her now that he was here. What's more, he had some thinking to do.

First thing, he needed to find out from Lydia's father if there was anything stopping him from testifying, because there wasn't a chance in fucking hell he was going to let the Hidalgos return to Mexico. Of course there also wasn't a chance in hell he was giving up Lydia to the Witness Protection Program either.

The phone vibrated in his pocket and he pulled it out. It was Darius asking him for a status. Rubbing the back of his neck, he gave another quick glance at Lydia, then took his time responding to Darius' text. He wasn't surprised by the immediate offer of help. He didn't expect anything less. He promised to call later.

He was tired. He had caught a little bit of shut eye on the flight from California to Dallas. The problem was all activity that had just gone on in California before he had left. He'd been up for almost two days and it was catching up with him.

Clint still needed to think through how best to protect Lydia. All of his big ideas that they should stay together were just assumptions, they hadn't really ever talked about a future together. Hell, they hadn't even really had much of a present together. All of their time together had been while she was recuperating in the hospital.

Scratch that. There were the first five days they had spent together. He looked down at her wrist and swore. He could still see a faint scar where the rope had bit into her flesh. Why hadn't they got there sooner? Seeing that small sign of abuse was all it took for him to flash back to the jungle.

"CLINT?"

He looked up and saw Beth standing over him. He must have fallen asleep. He looked at his watch. It hadn't been too long. She held out a cup of coffee.

"I owe you my life," he said taking the Styrofoam cup.

"I think you have that turned around." There was a hint of a smile in Beth's eyes that he was happy to see.

"Wanna tell me how you have been doing? Last I heard you and Lydia were doing some on-line education courses."

"Lydia's getting depressed. If we'd stayed in Mexico, Lydia would have finished her Masters by now. She had a job lined up and everything."

Clint couldn't help but feel a little bit of tension ease. He definitely supported Lydia taking a job in law enforcement but the Federal Ministerial Police had neon bulls-eyes on their backs. If he had his way, somehow he would figure out a way they didn't have to go into Witness Protection and she could take a job with the police near him in San Diego.

"Lydia won't talk about why she chose that line of work. Every time I ask, she just clams up."

Beth cocked her head and raised an eyebrow.

"Clams up, means she just doesn't say anything, she shuts her mouth," Clint explained.

"Ahhh. Sometimes I don't understand the American idioms. Before Papa got a good job at the accounting firm, we lived in a not so good part of Mexico City. We had neighbors, Angela and Herman. They were a young married couple who were gunned down walking home from the corner market. Angela was our babysitter. She was pregnant. He'd been questioned by the *policia* about another shooting. He hadn't said anything, but because they'd seen him talking the gangs killed him."

Clint could see how that would have convinced Lydia to commit herself to a career in law enforcement.

"Clint, have you checked into a hotel? You need to get some sleep."

"I'm just going to sleep here tonight."

"Mama said they gave her medication to sleep through the night. She's not going to wake up. You need to take care of yourself." He gave the young woman a half smile.

"Feeling a little more confident these days, are you?"

"With a few people. I still can't stand to be touched by a man. It breaks Papa's heart when I flinch away from him."

"Are you–"

"Yes. I already told you, am going to see the counselor. Both Lydia and I have talked to her." He looked from Beth down to where Lydia was lying in the bed.

"I'm glad."

"Don't be, it's not helping. Have you ever been to counseling?" Beth's chin jutted out, but her voice trembled. He wished he could take her into his arms and tell her it would be all right.

"Yes. There was a mission that went bad and it was mandatory."

"Did it help?"

Clint looked into her big black eyes and saw the doubt and hope.

"I didn't think so when I was going but now that I look back on it? Yeah. Yeah, I think it did help." Beth bit her lip.

"I've got to go. I'll see you in the morning."

"Thanks for the coffee."

She nodded, letting her dark hair cover her face and left.

He settled back in his seat while taking another sip of his coffee. It hadn't gotten any better since the last time he had been here. At least it wouldn't affect his ability to get to sleep. It was one of the first things he had learned in the military, how to sleep no matter the circumstances.

So TIRED. It felt like every one of her bones weighed fifty pounds. Even her fingers felt like they were made of lead. Damn, they'd drugged her again. She hated when they did that. It was always for her own good.

You need your rest, Lydia. It's the best medicine.

If she needed to rest, wouldn't she just go to sleep? She tried to shake her head to clear the fuzziness and that was when she saw him. Her heart tumbled over in her chest. Didn't it always when she saw this beautiful man?

Oh yeah, she'd seen him right as the drugs were taking affect. What had she said? She'd told him he needed to leave. That he didn't really know the real her. Lydia blushed. She'd always been a terrible liar. Clint had called her on it.

She traced the angles of his face with her eyes. He looked as tired as she felt. She reached across the white expanse of sheet, wishing she could hold his hand. Even that much effort wore her out, and she was fighting to keep her eyes open. At least the last thing she would see before she drifted off would be Clint Archer. Maybe she would dream of him.

THE FIRST THING Lydia noticed when she woke up was she felt better. She could feel the sunlight streaming in through the window and falling onto her face. She waited and then she heard it. Birds singing. She let out a sigh. It was going to be a better day. Then she grinned and turned her head and looked at the man sitting next to her.

He was looking at her. It had been the second day in the jungle when she had started to try to figure out what color his eyes were. Sometimes they were green, sometimes gray, in the right light they looked almost golden with flecks of turquoise. Today they were hazel.

"Hello." Her voice was raspy.

"Hi, Baby. You had me worried." His voice sounded like he chewed on gravel. It comforted her.

"I'm glad you're here."

"Didn't sound like it yesterday."

She shrugged. "I'm all over the board with this illness and being under the microscope at the safe house."

Clint pulled his chair even closer to the bed. He stroked her cheek with the back of his knuckles. "You're going to get better. Your father is going to testify. Life will get back to normal."

"What's normal?" She saw him struggle to answer. "I'm not trying to give you a trick question, I just mean I'm never going to have my old life back. I'm never going back to the woman I was before that day in the jungle."

"Baby, I–" She saw the pain on his face and stopped him.

"That came out wrong. I don't mean the whipping. I mean the kidnapping. I mean Papa conspiring with the cartel and then turning on them. Everything that led up to that day. I'm never going to work for the Federal Ministerial Police, even if I do return to Mexico City."

He cupped her cheek and gave her a steady look. "First, let's get one thing straight, you are not going back to Mexico City. You know there will always be people gunning for you. But if I met you before all of this happened, I want to be honest with you, it scared me to death you signed up for the Federal Ministerial Police."

She saw red, but then she took a deep breath, maybe she was reading this wrong.

"Clint?"

"Lydia, ever since you told me what you did back in Mexico City, I've been astounded by your bravery. But you never intended to stay a low level member of the Ministry, did you? You planned to fight for justice and take on the cartels, didn't you?" Lydia pulled away from the hand gripping her chin.

"Yes."

"That's why I was scared. I would have never asked you not to do something like that. How could I when my job is so dangerous, but it sure as hell scared me."

"I understand. Both of us want to serve our country, to

make them better places. Now I have to put my dream away." *And that hurt. It hurt a lot.*

She took a deep breath and gave him a big smile.

"But I don't want to talk about that. I want to talk about the fact that I'm feeling better and I have a handsome man who flew from California to visit me."

"I'm handsome, am I?" His eyes twinkled. She noticed the lines bracketing his mouth, and the days of dark blond scruff on his face. None of it diminished from the fact he was mouth-watering.

"Yep, you're handsome, in 'bad boy' sort of way. Not in a way that would appeal to a lady like *me*." Lydia couldn't maintain a straight face as she gave Clint a hard time. It felt good to be teasing and laughing. The last four months had been too stressful and depressing.

"I guess you're beautiful in the 'look but don't touch' sort of way. Not the type that would appeal to a down to earth type of guy like *me*." Clint's eyes warmed, and he picked up the hand that wasn't tethered to the IV and brushed his lips to her palm. She shuddered at the intimate sensation.

"Okay, let's get real a minute. You can't keep dropping in for visits each time I get a sniffle. I know you feel a sense of responsibility-"

Clint's palm covered her mouth before she even saw him move.

"Stop!" His palm was warm, the pressure didn't hurt, even though the look in his eyes was wild. He took one, then a second, and then a third calming breath.

"Lydia Rose, don't you fucking *dare* say I'm here because of some kind of misplaced sense of responsibility. You're too fucking smart for that. You might *try* to relegate it that way, but you *know* it's not. Are we clear? Are we?"

Looking at those glittering eyes that were now steely gray, she had no other choice but to nod.

He lifted his hand.

"Say it. Tell me what this is." His voice sounded like shards of rock being dragged over ice.

"I don't know exactly what it is. I've run this over and over in my head. I think it is the beginning of something that has the potential of being rare and special." Dammit, the tears were coming back. But again the hand was quicker than the eye, and he was holding hers, giving her comfort.

"Okay then. We're on the same page."

"When did you learn my middle name?"

"You mean you don't know mine?" His thumb traced patterns on her palm and had her stomach turning backflips.

"Clinton Anthony Archer. I like it."

"Why didn't they name you Rosa? I thought that would have been more Hispanic."

"Mama had an American friend named Rose. She thought it was nice."

"It is nice. Do you know what else is nice? Kissing."

The man was certifiable.

"Hey bed head, morning breath, hospital gown, and door not locked. How about you put off the whole kissing thing until next spring?" Clint was out of his chair and leaning over the bedrail looking into her eyes.

"I've dreamed about kissing you for damn near four months. You have the most delectable lips." He wasn't looking in her eyes anymore, he was focused on her mouth and he looked hungry. He wasn't kidding. *Oh God, she wanted this so badly, but she wanted to look beautiful for him.*

"You take my breath away."

"I will if you kiss me."

His thumb grazed her bottom lip, parting them. "You're not going to stop me, Lydia."

Ever so slowly, he bent forward. She trembled, but he caught her, his right hand easing behind her neck, slipping into her hair and angling her head just right so their lips could meet in a soft sigh of hello.

He massaged her scalp as he brushed back and forth until she was following his lead, anxious to find out where the magic would lead. He didn't rush a thing, letting her get used to the heat and texture, and then she flowered open, needing more. He didn't rush the invitation, instead he gently parted her further, the hand that had been holding her chin splayed along her jaw and she rubbed against the strength of him.

He surrounded her in caring, tears pricked the back of her eyes. Her breasts swelled. She pushed against his chest and demanded more. His tongue swept inside, and soon he was thrusting in the rhythm she desired, wanted, needed. She heard a sound and realized it was her.

Clint soothed her, tracing her cheek with his calloused fingertips, caressing her hair down her back.

"Shhhh, I have you." His forehead rested against hers, and she could finally open her eyes. Passion turned his to emerald green. Now she knew her favorite color.

IT'D BEEN TWO WEEKS, and she was still mooning over one damn kiss. *Seriously girlfriend, you need your head examined.*

"So what's the good word Dr. Woods? Do I get to leave?" It wasn't like she had anything great to look forward to when she left. According to the US Marshalls they were still looking at least another six weeks at the safe house.

"I need a promise from you Lydia, you need to actually to follow my directive when you leave this time. You ignored the symptoms and allowed yourself to come down with another case of pneumonia. You didn't need to. It didn't need to get to this point. You're a smart woman? You never told me why."

"Is this under doctor and patient privilege?" Lydia was sitting up in the bed, and gave the doctor a steady look.

"If that's the only way you'll tell me and assure me you'll take care of yourself, then yes."

"Papa is hanging on by a thread. He feels so much guilt about what happened to Beth and me, whenever he is reminded of it, he....he." Lydia couldn't say it. It was a sin.

"Lydia, talk to me." The doctor's eyes were so compassionate. She was a good woman, someone Lydia had come to admire and trust.

"He took a bunch of pills. Mama found him before it was too late. She got him to throw up. We didn't tell the Marshalls. We took care of it. If he thought I was getting sick again, it would have been too much for him."

"Jesus. You know he needs help," she breathed out.

"I know. But if the Marshalls find out, they might put him in some kind of institution until the trial. Mama hasn't left his side. We keep telling him that he would be leaving all of us when we needed him the most." Lydia clutched the handrail at the side of her bed, wincing when she tugged against the IV in her hand.

"Lydia, you can't be living like that. So once again you hid the fact you were getting ill to your detriment."

Lydia looked down, unable to face the recrimination in the doctor's eyes.

"In some ways, staying at the hospital has been a Godsend."

"Fine, I'll have you stay longer."

"It's too much to ask of my mother. I need to go back. I can see the toll it has taken on her. I need to get back to her."

"Stress isn't good for you. You need rest."

"Doctor, you told me that my recovery has been remarkable."

"That's because you've had so much rest. Some of the visitors you've had didn't hurt either." Dr. Wood's eyes sparkled. Lydia laughed and the two women were definitely on the same page.

"Clint is back in California. He won't be back."

"Oh, I think you're reading that wrong. He'll be back."

"He's taken all the time off he can," Lydia assured her doctor. "It doesn't matter anyway, there's not a future for us. I asked him to leave for good."

The door opened, and Beth walked in with a man Lydia didn't recognize.

"Where's Ed?" Lydia asked, referring to Edward Lasson, the US Marshall who was guarding Lydia while she had been in the hospital.

"His wife is sick. This is Nelson Barber," Beth grinned. "Ed called and told me he was okay, also he has all of the correct identification."

"Oh, I hope Ed's wife is okay." Lydia heard about Carmella and really liked everything she had heard about her. Beth bit her lip.

"What?"

"Ed didn't sound like himself. He sounded really

upset. I think she's really sick."

"He has plenty of vacation to take care of his wife," Nelson said easily. "I just wanted to let you know that I would be guarding your door for the next twenty-four to forty-eight hours." He let himself out of the room.

"Lydia, I'll check on you tomorrow, but I think I should be able to release you the day after that."

Lydia smiled.

"That's really good news. I've missed her," Beth said. Lydia looked at her sister, and realized her mother wasn't the only one who had been feeling the strain. She held out her hand to Beth.

"I'll let you two visit. Remember, this time if you feel any of your symptoms coming back, you *have* to tell us immediately."

"I promise."

"I'll be dragging her into your office. This won't happen again." Beth gave Lydia a dark look. Her little sister looked fierce.

"I promise *both* of you. I won't backslide again." Beth wrapped her in a tight hug. For the first time Lydia realized how much she scared her. Dammit, she should never have let it get this far, it was like she was squeezed between a rock and a hard place.

She heard the door close behind the doctor, and then she pushed Beth back so she could look into her face.

"Okay, I want to hear everything. Tell me what's been going on."

"It's been fine."

"Sit your butt in that chair and tell me everything. If you leave anything out, I'll know, and you will be in big trouble."

Beth sat down and Lydia listened.

LYDIA SLAMMED DOWN HER E-READER. She'd thought it would be a breeze to comprehend the textbook in English. She was wrong. Dammit, getting her Master's degree in the United States would take her twice as long. She was fluent in English, she was a 4.0 student at the University in Mexico, but the course work was just different enough that her degree was slipping away.

Then she had to figure out what she would do with it when she obtained it. Hell, she didn't even know where she would be, or who she would be. She heard horror stories about the Witness Protection Program where they wouldn't let you work in the field you had studied for. She hated this.

"Damn you, Papa!"

She clapped her hand over her mouth. Had she really said that? She thought about what Beth said. Her little sister was so worried about her parents, that she was making herself ill when she should really be trying to heal. *She wouldn't have to heal if her father hadn't started working for the cartel.*

All the time Lydia had been studying to fight the corruption in her country her father had been helping them to launder money. Fine, she'd been killing herself to graduate early and getting a double major, but how could she have been so blind? She wasn't sure what made her sicker, her father's actions or her own stupidity. He might have eventually done the right thing and went to the authorities, but that he had even done it for a day, ruined every ideal she had ever held about her father.

Everything Beth had told her sounded like Papa was finally convinced to testify. That meant Witness

Protection. Lydia thought about Clint. Then her heart melted. Actually melted. The idea of not seeing Clint Anthony Archer again was not to be born.

She traced the back of her e-reader. What was the point of even studying? She took a deep breath and then another. Her lungs were doing much better. She was feeling so much stronger. She eyed the closet holding the clothes Beth brought for her to wear home. Wouldn't it be great to just walk out of here? Just leave?

Maybe then she could have the life *she* wanted. Nope, the government would never allow it. Clint would never stop serving his country. Her head was in the clouds. There had to be a way. Life would never be this unfair!

"Sell it somewhere else, Hidalgo." *Great, now she was talking to herself.*

She more than anyone on Earth knew life wasn't fair and she had the scars to prove it. She picked up her e-reader. Dammit. But she was going to figure a way out of this mess.

She looked over at the nightstand and considered getting out her computer. Maybe she could do a little more hacking, a little more probing into the life of one Alfonso Guzman. Her father might be reconsidering testifying, but there was no way in hell she was going to let those bastards win. But she knew her brain wasn't firing on all cylinders and she couldn't afford to be caught. There were too many firewalls that she needed to breach. She'd need to stick with studying right now. Tomorrow would be a better day for hacking.

She settled in to read more about the *Trends in Computer Networks and Security*, if nothing else it would help her get the rest that the doctor was always saying she needed.

5

She barely heard him as Nelson came to her bedside. But she saw the syringe he was pocketing. Every sense in her body went on high alert.

Oh God!

She looked at her IV and realized she probably had only a few moments. If she screamed, he might kill her outright. She needed him to leave the room. Lydia turned her hand and pinched the tube so it stopped the flow of liquid. She watched him leave through her lashes. Maybe she was wrong, but she knew she wasn't.

Reaching for the call button for the nurse, she found it cut. Dammit, this was real! Yanking the IV out of the back of her hand, Lydia screamed at the top of her lungs.

This time Clint wasn't alone when he arrived in Dallas. He was surrounded by his team.

"You have point on this mission, Clint. You know the situation," Mason whispered to him.

Clint looked over at Mason and gave him a tight smile. They had commandeered one of the conference rooms at the hospital. Peter Grogan, the man who ran the Dallas office of the US Marshall Service, was in the room with them. He had a file in front of him.

"I'm not happy about this. This is something that we should take care of, you should not be involved." Grogan was sitting at the head of the table; it was clear that he was used to being in charge.

Mason didn't say anything, he just stared at the man. It was a good tactic, he shifted in his seat and finally continued to talk.

"I haven't been given a choice. Lieutenant, you and your team have now been given total control of the Hidalgos' safety." He sighed.

"The first thing we need is to better understand what happened. How were your people compromised?" Mason was relaxed and spoke quietly, while Clint wanted to take the man outside and beat the hell out of him for his incompetence.

"Nelson Barber has worked for us for over three years. When he applied everything checked out. He went through a rocky divorce a year ago and we found out he became a financial risk."

"Don't you monitor for that type of thing?" Mason asked calmly.

"We do."

Again, Mason didn't say anything.

"Obviously, it slipped through the cracks. Barber hasn't been found." Grogan pushed one of the files over to Mason. "Here is everything we have on Barber. Apparently we missed a lot. His brother was in on this too. He owns a janitorial company and has ex-cons and drug dealers on his payroll, which we're sure Barber was using to do some of his dirty work. They're actually paying these people and taking out taxes!"

He slapped his hand against the table.

This was going downhill fast. They still needed more information and cooperation, and having Grogan all upset wasn't going to help matters.

"How's Ed doing?" Clint asked, trying to help calm the man down.

"He's going to be fine. Barber was using one of his old snitches to keep Ed locked up so he could take the call from Beth. The snitch, who was on his brother's payroll by the way, got nervous and left Ed in the motel room. We found him from his phone's GPS. He's going to make a full recovery. If Lydia hadn't foiled this bastard's murder attempt, she and Ed would both be dead."

Clint's gut clenched. Yeah, it was great Ed was okay, but he didn't want to even think about Lydia not waking up when she did.

"So at this point you haven't told the parents anything, correct?" Clint asked.

"That's correct. Unfortunately, the sisters talked before we could stop them, so Beth knows what happened. But we asked them to keep it from their parents."

"That's probably going to be for the best anyway," Clint said thinking out loud.

"Why, what do you have in mind?" Grogan asked.

"Actually Sir, we don't have to tell you anything more. You've provided us with all of the information we need," Mason said. He stood and opened the door of the conference room. "We're going to discuss our next steps, and when we need your cooperation we'll contact you."

Grogan looked at all of the men in the room. "I deeply

regret what happened on my watch. I'm doing a full investigation of my team. Barber's immediate supervisor is on suspension. Going forward I won't be delegating a damn thing regarding this case. You can reach me day or night. You need it, it's yours."

"I appreciate that." Mason shook the hand offered to him. After the door closed he turned back to his men.

"Clint's closest to this whole situation, it's his woman who was almost killed. I'm putting him in charge of this op. Does anyone have any problems with that?"

"As long as the operation entails bringing her pretty ass back to San Diego where we can keep her under lock and key, I don't have any problems." Drake's Southern drawl soothed Clint as much as his words did.

"Trust me, it was definitely my first inclination." Clint grinned over at his friend.

"Great. We're done here. Let's get us some Texas Barbeque." Drake started to get up from his seat.

"Sit down, Avery," Mason said to his second-in-command. "This is the reason you're not in charge when a woman's life is on the line, you go all caveman and then the bad guys win."

"That's corn fed bullshit, Mason. You went all sorts of caveman when Sophia was in trouble and it was a damn good thing you did. You kept her safe dude, and it's the same thing we need to do this time."

Clint unclenched his fists and brought his palms to the table. "Drake, we have multiple priorities. Make no mistake keeping Lydia unharmed is priority number one."

"I never doubted it, Clint," Drake said with a wink. "I'm thinking Dickey's. I hear their barbeque sauce is the best."

"We're not leaving to get barbeque. This is going to be

a complicated op," Clint said, beginning to get frustrated with his friend.

"So we take the brisket to go, pick up Lydia and fly back to Cali."

"Be fucking serious for a minute!" Clint pointed at Drake. "Put your ass back down in your seat."

"Are you sure you want him running this op, Mason? It seems to me he doesn't have the people skills," Drake said as he plopped down into the leather seat.

"Look, we have an opportunity to flush out who was pulling Barber's strings. This is a chance for us to take down the cartel and hopefully Alfonso Guzman." Clint tried to sound reasonable but Drake made it difficult.

"Grogan said Barber is gone. So if I'm reading this right the only way this works if use Lydia as bait. Are you out of your fucking mind?" Drake yelled incredulously. "Mason, are you good with this shit, because if you are I want to know when the fucking pod people came and took over the two of you."

"Fuck you, Drake!" Clint hit his fist on the conference room table. Out of the corner of his eye he saw Finn and Darius were watching him closely. He knew that they agreed with Drake, but were letting him take the lead...for now. "I already told you Lydia's safety was priority number one."

"You go fuck yourself, Archer. Lydia is a non-combattant. What's more, that woman has gone through more than anyone should ever have to live through. She's paid her dues and now is the time to get out the cotton wool. I won't have it. She is not going to be used by anyone, especially not by the man who I thought loved her."

"You're out of line," Mason said quietly.

"Mason, you can't seriously condone this shit."

"I said, you need to hear what the man has to say." Drake looked from Mason to Clint, who just stared at him.

"Fine. Talk."

"Drake, you know me. At least hear me out like Finn and Dare are willing to do." Clint looked at the four men seated around the table. Drake might have been the one who was talking, but he knew Finn and Darius felt the same way. As it should be. No man with a heart should want to use Lydia Hidalgo as bait.

"So can you explain it to all of us now? I know you've talked to Lydia, and you've come away with a potential plan, but I really haven't liked it either. Can you lay it out for us?" Mason asked.

Clint rested his arms against the granite table top and sighed.

"Lydia was getting her master's degree in computer science. She already had a double major in computer science and criminal justice. She intended to go to work for the Federal Ministerial Police. She's seen the devastation that the drug cartels wreaked on her country and she wanted to fight against them."

"She's a computer geek? Like you?" That was from Finn who was looking at him in amazement.

"She's so much more than just a computer *geek*. She tried to explain to me how she has this boring degree, but it has a little extra emphasis on cyber-crimes. She's so full of shit. When we really got to talking, I realized just how good she is. Then I saw what she could do on a computer —pure magic. Plus, she has a network of people that tells me she's been at this for quite a long time. Long before college. She's fucking amazing."

"Been doing a little computer canoodling, have you?" Darius teased.

"She's been sick. Our boy needed to figure out some kind of way to canoodle," Finn said grinning broadly.

"Anyway," Clint said raising his hands. "When this attempt on her life was made, even though it was made by a US Marshall, it still showed any and all Hidalgos are targets. We figured Lydia was the easiest to get to because she wasn't at the safe house. She wanted to use that. She wants to use herself as bait so we can flush out the bad guys."

"Again, I say no. Fuck, no!" Drake crossed his arms, leaned back in his chair and plopped his boots onto the table top.

"You wouldn't last two minutes with her. She'd hand you your dick, Drake." Clint grinned to himself, imagining Drake trying to tell Lydia what to do.

"You're pussy-whipped my friend."

"Call *me* whatever you want. But you have to call *her*, brave, and right."

"Doesn't mean it's going to happen."

Finn chuckled. Clint couldn't blame him. Drake was damn near pouting.

"Okay, now you understand why the woman is so adamant she participate in taking these bastards down. And of course I'm not going to allow her to use herself as bait. *But*, I am going to have her be a very active participant in finding a way to give her life back. We have to cut the head off this cartel and it's Alfonso Guzman."

"She must've been incensed when she found out her dad was working with the cartel," Darius said as he perused the file Grogan had left.

"That's another thing that's so impressive. She is loyal

to a fault. I'm positive she's pissed, but she barely says a word against her father." Clint caught glimpses of Lydia's anger, but she almost always tamped it down. "It doesn't really matter, does it? In the end, he tried to do the right thing."

"I wonder how much of it was due to Lydia." Darius turned over one of the papers in the file and started skimming the next.

"I don't think she had any idea what he was into. But I think it was probably because of her he tried to make things right," Clint agreed.

"Okay, she's part of the team. Now what do we do to make sure that absolutely nothing fucking happens to harm one fucking hair on her fucking head?" Everybody stared at Drake.

"How do you really feel?" Finn finally asked.

"Step one is to split up the family. They are expecting we will be keeping them together, and that stops immediately." Clint pressed a button on his computer, and his screen displayed on the wall. It showed a map of the US, in the middle of Texas was a star.

"Okay, so does each one of them go with one of us?" Drake asked. "Who goes where?"

"We have to keep Mr. Hidalgo with the US Marshalls. But, they will have one of you with them. Since he's going to be testifying the Marshalls wouldn't let him out of their sight. Beth will be the one staying in Texas. She's going to San Antonio."

"So four of us are going to be utilized?" Darius asked.

"Negative," Mason answered. "Captain Hale has a mission that requires three of us to ship out in forty-eight hours. Clint can explain how this will work."

"Mason has been thinking of bringing a sixth person

onto our team, and this is an opportunity to test him out. His name is Jack Preston." Clint smiled when even Drake gave a nod of approval.

"Jack's family has a ranch in San Antonio. Beth is going to go with him. Finn, you're going to be attached to Mr. and Mrs. Hidalgo."

"You're not splitting them up?"

"Lydia said it would be too much of a strain on her mom if she was separated from her dad. She'd know. You'll be going to Chicago."

"Where are you and Lydia heading?"

"We're going to a safe house in Tampa. Now, let's start working out the details."

BETH WALKED into the hospital room where Lydia and her parents were waiting.

"My Baby, come here." Beth was swept up into her mother's arms. Lydia was sitting in the chair by the window, her dad stood next to her, looking grim.

"I don't like this," he said in Spanish.

"English, Papa."

"It doesn't matter, they're taking both of my babies from me," Lydia's mother said tearfully. She hugged Beth closer. "Where are you going my daughter?"

"I can't tell you."

"Please Beth," their mother started to cry. Beth looked over her mother's shoulder at Lydia with a helpless look on her face.

"Mama, you know the rules. This is to keep us safe." Lydia got up from the chair slowly, and wrapped her arms around the two women who meant the world to her.

"I can't stand the thought of being separated from my babies."

"They said we could call one another," Lydia reminded her. She brushed a kiss against her mother's cheek.

"And you're barely out of a hospital bed. Who's going to take care of you?" For the first time since she entered the room, there was a glimmer of a smile on Beth's face.

"Lydia is going with Clint Archer. He's going to be taking care of her."

"He is?" Her mother pulled back so she could look at Lydia. "Where are you going?" Both girls groaned.

"Mama, I can't tell you that."

"Gloria, my love, ask your daughters a different question." Lydia looked over her shoulder and realized her father hadn't moved from his spot near the window. He still looked morose.

"I would tell you where we were going if I knew."

Beth laughed. "That's probably why they haven't told you yet, Mama."

"Papa, are you all right?" Lydia asked.

"Oh sure I'm just fine. My daughter was almost murdered, now we are being separated. It is still likely that even if I testify, we will all be killed. Why wouldn't I be all right?"

"Ricardo! That is not going to happen. You must have faith in God."

"God is falling down on the job, Gloria."

Her mother crossed herself.

"Please, don't fight," Beth begged.

"God saved Lydia. We'll all be protected. I'll not hear this blasphemy anymore." Her father shrank before her very eyes. He walked over to them, and put his arms around his little family.

"I am sorry my love. You are right. All will be well."

"I have to go." Their father took Beth into his arms and hugged her tight, and Beth burst into tears. He handed her off to Lydia.

"Do what they say. They will protect you with their lives." Beth wiped her eyes and looked at her sister.

"Please don't let this opportunity go to waste," Beth said looking pointedly at Lydia. "You deserve all the happiness in the world." Lydia held onto Beth just a little longer.

"You deserve happiness too, Beth. I love you."

6

"You've never been on a road trip?"

Clint looked at her like she said she never heard of peanut butter.

"We lived in the city. Sometimes not in the best part of the city. When we went on holiday, it was to our grandparents' in the country. It was an hour north. Does that count?"

"No! You have to stop at gas stations and buy junk food. You have to eat at greasy spoons. You have to stop at tourist traps."

"I understood gas stations and junk food. What is a greasy spoon and a tourist trap?" Clint opened the passenger door of the black SUV and helped her inside. He made sure she was buckled in.

"Are you comfortable? Here is how you lower your seat back. Why don't you get some rest before we get to the first greasy spoon?"

"What is a greasy spoon?" Lydia asked as Clint got into the driver's seat.

"It has to be experienced sweetheart." He pulled out of

the hotel parking lot. She had been taken by ambulance to the hotel hours earlier, in order to throw any potential pursuers off track. Currently she was wearing a scarf around her head, sunglasses, and clothes two sizes too big for her.

Somehow Clint had morphed into a stereotypical suburban husband. It must have been the polo shirt and khaki pants, or it could have been the way he was carrying himself. But he no longer looked like the warrior she knew him to be.

"Tampa, huh? How long to get there?"

"We're going to take it slow. We'll get there in three days. I want to make sure we take it easy." They were already on the freeway and he was going eighty miles an hour.

"Ummm, Clint? What part of taking it slow are you subscribing too?"

He looked at her. She pointed to the speedometer and he looked at it and smiled.

"I meant we were going to stop often so you could rest. I have us booked at three different hotels on the way to Florida." "Lydia, you have to be tired, why don't you take a nap."

"I want to know where all of my family went." Clint reached over without looking and grasped her hand. He pulled it towards him and rested it on his thigh. It felt good there. The man was all muscle. She savored the warmth. She looked up at his face. He wasn't smiling anymore; he was grimacing. She smiled. Served him right for putting her hand there.

"Lydia, protocol states we can't tell you where they went." He threaded his fingers through hers. "I can tell you Finn went with your parents."

"Who went with Beth?"

"She's in safe hands."

"You mean she isn't with one of your men?" For the first time in forever Lydia found herself struggling for air.

"She's with another Navy SEAL. He's someone I respect and admire." She tried to yank her hand away, but he wouldn't let her.

"I don't care. He's a stranger. How could you allow that?" She heard her voice rise, and it sounded so loud in the small confines of the vehicle.

"He's the right man for the job. You know how I feel about your sister, Lydia. I would never trust her with anyone that wasn't the best. He will defend her with his life."

"But she is too fragile. She still doesn't trust people, especially men. I was depending on the fact that it would be one of your men. She knows all of you. After what we went through in the jungle, she could handle being with one of you."

"I was there when Jack and Beth met. It was fine. He handled her perfectly. I can't tell you the exact location of where they're going. But what I can tell you is it's a ranch and his mother is there."

Lydia shut her mouth on the next words she was about to say. She couldn't have heard Clint correctly. She looked at him again, and saw him nodding his head.

"Yep, his mom. Seriously Lydia, Beth is going to be fine. Things will work out."

She dropped her head back onto the seat.

Fine. What a weird concept. She'd left *fine* back in the dust almost half a year ago.

HE HATED to wake her up. Hell she'd looked healthier that first day back in the jungle. She might have even looked better the second day when the infection started to grab hold. She'd probably weighed fifteen pounds more then. Of course either way she was beautiful.

They'd been travelling on I-20 for hours and finally arrived in Shreveport, Louisiana. Clint had two sets of reservations waiting for them. One was at one of the riverboat casinos under the alias he used to rent the SUV. There was another reservation he made at a little bed and breakfast under another alias the US Marshalls never heard about.

He pulled into the dark and crowded parking lot of the riverboat casino.

"I fucking love, Finn," he muttered. He stopped the SUV, got out and removed the traffic cone from the parking spot beside the RV in spot EE25. He got back into his car and pulled into the now empty spot. Lydia still hadn't stirred.

Clint found the keys to the vehicle on the top of the tire in the rear left wheel well, right where they had it planned. He checked out the interior of the well-appointed motor home before bringing in their things from the trunk of the SUV. When he was done, he opened the passenger side door and traced his fingers down the side of Lydia's cheek.

"What?" Her eyes opened slowly. "Hi Clint." She smiled.

"Hi Baby. How're you feeling? Are you about ready for a restroom? For dinner?"

"Soon. I would like to get out and stretch." He reached over and unbuckled her seat belt, and then held out his hand to help her out of the car. Her first steps were unsteady.

"Dammit!"

"Why don't you swear in Spanish?"

"Are you trying to divert my attention from the fact I can barely walk?" Clint supported Lydia as she took shaky steps in the parking lot.

"A little bit. But I am curious about why your English is so good, hell you even swear in it."

"Trust me, it isn't that good. I'm struggling with the Computer Science texts in English and it's killing me. I thought I would just breeze through. I have a friend of mine in the University, and she's originally from Russia, but she went to high school in France. When she was in class, I would see her listening to the professor speaking in Spanish, but she would be writing in French, because that is the language she first started to study computers in. She was brilliant."

Clint shook his head, as he guided her back towards the RV. He could feel her weakening. "I can read and write in English and Spanish. I can speak and understand some Farsi and Arabic, but that's it for me. Do you speak any more than English and Spanish?"

"Portuguese. My grandfather was from Brazil, and some German. A little Japanese. Dammit," she said as she stumbled. Clint swung her up into his arms.

"What are you doing?"

"Exactly what I've been wanting to do. I love being able to hold you. Now tell me why you swear in English and not in Spanish." He headed towards the RV.

"Because Mama and Papa didn't understand what I was saying when I swore in English." He grinned.

"I thought it was some sort of big linguistic trial you

put yourself through, instead you were being a normal kid. I love it." He opened the door of the RV.

"Clint, this isn't our vehicle. Have you become a car thief?"

"Does this look like a Corvette? A Ferrari? A Lamborghini?"

"Nope, looks like a mansion on wheels. Maybe a couple of years old, but my God. Oh…. This is part of our cover. Damn, I think you being a car thief and us driving a Ferrari would be more fun." He stepped up into the RV and gently deposited her into the big and comfortable chair beside the driver's seat.

"I'll remember that and when we're done with all of this we'll have to take a *real* road trip. You would love to go driving on the Pacific Coast Highway in a convertible. In the meantime, I promised you a bathroom and dinner at a greasy spoon." He got into the driver's seat and started the engine. The RV roared to life. He adjusted the mirrors, and started backing out of the parking space. Shit, a Humvee seemed like a Fiat compared to this boat.

HE SHOULD NEVER HAVE LET her talk him into stopping at the alligator farm and petting zoo. It served him right, he had pointed it out as a tourist trap and as soon as he did she had wanted to check it out. He put his foot down when she said she wanted to do the zip line and got them the hell out of there. She was trembling with exhaustion, and he was kicking his ass by the time the time they pulled into Shreveport, Louisiana.

He was tempted to pull over at a rest stop and make her go to bed in the RV, but the idea of sitting on the side of a road a rest stop made him too damn twitchy. Lydia wanted to eat dinner at a restaurant but he nixed the idea, instead saying they were going to order room service when they got to their hotel room.

Since they were going everywhere as a couple, there was one king sized bed. He got her tucked in and then went out on the balcony and called Darius.

"Clint, what's wrong?" He heard the sound of a helicopter.

"Can you talk?"

"For a minute. What's wrong?"

"Lydia. I think she needs to be in the hospital. She's so weak. She's only been awake for three hours in the last twenty-four. She can barely walk."

"Clint, this is the first real day out of the hospital. They wouldn't have let her out if she wasn't ready to leave. Every single day she'll get better. But make sure she doesn't push herself."

"She's so frustrated."

"It's going to be up to you to make sure that she doesn't overexert herself. You sit on her if you have to, but make sure she really gives her body a chance to recover this time. It's clear she's been putting her parent's welfare above her own. That shit has got to stop. While you two are in hiding should be the perfect time for her to really recover."

Clint leaned against the rail and looked out over the Red River. Darius was right. He could make sure she finally took the time to recover properly. Her dad wasn't due to testify for six weeks. Hell, she didn't even need to be there for that. The trial and his testimony could go on for weeks.

"Thanks, Dare."

"You're welcome. I've got to go."

"Stay safe."

"Always."

Clint went back into the room. He already pulled pillows and blankets to sleep on the floor. For one brief second considered the small sofa, but he would have ended up a pretzel in the morning. He quietly made use of the bathroom, and came out into the darkened bedroom.

"Clint?"

"Is there something you need, Baby?" He saw Lydia propped up on her elbow. "Are you hungry? You didn't eat anything."

"No, I'm fine."

"I'm sorry I woke you. Go back to sleep." He knelt down on the rug he had positioned between the bed and the door.

"What are you doing?"

"Going to sleep?'"

"There?" He heard an odd note in her voice.

"Yeah."

"Why would you do that? It's a huge bed."

"I'm used to sleeping on the ground. I've got a rug, blankets and a pillow. This is heaven."

"Oh." He watched as she lowered herself back down. Through the gauzy curtains the moonlight highlighted her face. She looked hurt.

"Lydia, what's wrong?"

"Nothing." God, no phrase in the world was more likely to set off alarm bells than asking a woman if something was wrong and her saying 'nothing'.

He got up from the floor and went to the bed.

"Baby, what's wrong? Please tell me."

She was curled on her side, and as he approached she

rolled to the other side, away from him, hugging the edge of the bed. Oh yeah, something was definitely wrong. *I'm an idiot.*

"Lydia, I wanted to sleep in the bed with you. I wanted to hold you, like we had in the jungle, but it just didn't seem right. And you're sick. I thought it would be best if I slept on the floor."

She didn't move. Yep, she was either angry or hurt, or maybe both.

"Lydia?"

"Lydia, I'm sorry."

"It's no big deal."

He looked at her there, curled up in the fetal position. Had he just heard a hint of tears in her voice? He touched her shoulder and she didn't move.

Fuck it! In for a penny, in for a pound.

He got up and threw back the covers, and made himself comfortable in the middle of the bed. Lydia trembled and he wasn't having any of it. He reached around her waist and hauled her up close to him and buried his nose in her soft and shiny curls. She smelled like sunshine. She was just what he needed.

She kept her legs up close to her chest with her arms wrapped around them. "Lydia, I wasn't rejecting you baby. This is really where I wanted to be."

He felt her body loosen. He nuzzled the side of her neck, and he smoothed his hands down her arms until she let go. He tangled his legs with hers, so she was soon spooned against him. He twisted a little so his aching erection wasn't pressed against her bottom. This was not about sex, this was about closeness and comfort.

"I don't want to force you to do something you don't

want to do," she said in a voice so soft he strained to hear it.

"You're kidding, right?"

She jerked and her body started to go rigid.

"Hey, I was making a joke. What's going on, baby?"

"Nothing. Everything. I think it is all catching up to me. I really didn't want to go back to the safe house, but I feel guilty for feeling that way."

"There's no reason for you to feel guilty, it's totally understandable."

She rolled over and looked at him, her face traced with tears.

"I love my parents. I do! So much. But–" She stopped short.

"You've been strong for so many people for so long. It would be my honor if you would lean on me for a little while."

"Being on the run with you—leaning on you—is not how I envisioned our time together. If we were ever lucky enough to meet when this Witness Protection Program wasn't looming over our heads, I was hoping to be on equal footing."

She rested her fists against his chest. He could see the anguish on her face and it killed him. He took one of her hands coaxed it open, and rested it against his flesh. She looked up at him with a question in her eyes.

The fact is you do have to rely on me for the next couple of weeks while we are in hiding and you recuperate. But in no way does that make you diminished in my eyes."

She pushed against him. He covered her hand and kept his other against her back so she continued to stay in his arms.

"I'm not letting you go. Having you sleep next to me is something I've dreamed about for months. I am humbled at the idea of being able to care for you, only this time knowing you *will* get well, this isn't life and death. It's a dream come true. I've faced life and death many times, but I've never been as scared as when I thought you were going to die."

Her beautiful brown eyes filled with more tears as she looked up at him. "You saved me, Clint. Not just by carrying me and caring for me. But it was your will that made me fight to live."

He shuddered, even now the terror could slice through him too easily at odd times, and he would be back there thinking she was dead. He brushed the tears from her face. "I'm glad I gave you a reason to fight to live. Now fight hard to get well and to get well fast. Because when you're well I want to hold you, press you against me, and feel your naked flesh slide against mine."

"That's what I want. I want it right now." Her hand slid up his chest, around his neck, and threaded through his hair kneading his scalp. She wrapped her other arm around his torso bringing them chest to breast.

She was wearing a well-worn Hello Kitty sleep shirt. When she'd gotten into bed her breasts had been lovingly outlined, and he could even make out her bikini panties.

"Lydia, you're killing me."

"Good."

"Not good. You need your rest." She growled. The woman actually growled, and it had to be the sexiest thing he ever heard.

"If I hear one more person say I need rest I'm going to pluck out their nipple hairs."

He burst out laughing as he winced. At least she hadn't talked about hair below the belt buckle.

"Easy there. I'm sorry I mentioned rest. I won't do it again. At least not tonight."

"You better not do it ever again if you know what's good for you." She shifted to the right, dragging her breasts against him. Her pebbled nipples rasping against his chest. It took everything he had not to press his aroused flesh against her pelvis.

"Lydia, you're making me lose my mind."

"Good. You have to admit, this is so much better than you sleeping on the floor or me *resting*," she whispered the words softly into his ear before scraping her teeth against his neck. He trembled and felt her tremble. How much was from fatigue, and how much was from passion?

"Lydia, morning is going to come pretty early and I drove most of the day." He let his voice drift off.

"Bullshit, you're trying to get me to go to sleep. I can't sleep. I'm too wound up. Make love to me." He wanted to. More than anything in the world, he wanted to spend hours exploring all the ways they could pleasure one another. But he remembered his conversation with Darius, and knew his priority was to help her get healthy.

"Baby, let me hold you. I won't use the 'R' word, I promise. We'll just lay here. But you just got out of the hospital. I'm not going to do anything except hold you tonight."

"Clint, I just got done sleeping for eight hours. I'm a grown woman and I know my own mind. Not only are you disrespecting me, you're hurting me."

He listened to her, but he just couldn't wrap his head around her words. She had just been in the hospital. Then he heard her whimper and all of his resolve went out the window. He knew he couldn't leave her in need.

"Shhhh, I have you."

"Thank God."

"Let's go slow. I need to savor every moment with you."

She pushed back from him and before he had a chance to blink, her shirt was over her head and on the floor. She twisted and turned the lamp on. He gulped.

"You're not shy."

"Not where your body is concerned. I've wanted to see you up close and personal for months."

IT WASN'T until he visited the hospital that Lydia really *looked* at Clint, and when she had, *Oh. My. God.* The man was amazing. Up until then she only looked at his face, his eyes, his soul. He had been something sent from heaven, a savior, someone to hang on to.

The first time in the hospital, she wrestled with the idea of the man who had been in the jungle with her now being with her in a real life setting. She wanted to eat him up with a spoon. It was totally inappropriate. He'd been there as a friend, as someone who rescued her and wanted to check in on her well-being. What's more, she'd been sick and shouldn't let her hormones run wild. But she wasn't the only one salivating. Every time Clint was in her room, the nurses seemed to have to check her vitals a hell of a lot more often. Now she had him right where she wanted, with his shirt off, sharing a bed with her. *Wasn't she a lucky girl?* She sat up.

"You're gorgeous." His big hands encircled her waist and slowly coasted upwards until they cupped her breasts.

She grabbed his wrists and pulled him away from her aching flesh.

"You'll get your turn, I promise. But please, I'm begging you, me first." She held her breath while she waited, he must have seen something in her expression.

"Baby, if I can't go first, can't we do it together?"

"I really need this."

After long moments she saw Clint got with the program, because he rolled onto his back, propped up on both elbows, looking up at her with a seductive smile.

"Do your worst."

"How about I do my best?" She reached out to touch him, but her hand hovered over him afraid to actually touch. The man had washboard abs. He gently gripped her wrist and placed her hand on his chest.

"Don't tease Lydia, I need your touch." Heat and strength were wrapped in soft suede. She opened her hand so her palm could press against all of that glorious flesh. She needed more, in a heartbeat, she found herself doing exactly what he said so long ago, sliding her naked flesh against his.

He groaned; she sighed. "So good, this feels so good, Clint."

She arched up like a cat, dragging her breasts against his chest so she could get closer to his mouth. It was time for another kiss. She prayed it would be as good as the one in the hospital. She didn't see how it could be, but at least her breath would be better.

"What are you grinning about?" Clint asked through gritted teeth. "Because Baby you're killing me."

She took advantage of his open mouth, meshing her mouth to his. They floated downwards, so he was lying flat on the pillows. His hands skimmed up her back, until his fingers tangled in her hair. She thought she would be in charge, but as soon as their lips met the kiss took over.

Who didn't matter as much as the velvet sensation of tongues languidly tasting. The pleasure of plush lips pressed against soft, firm masculine lips was sublime. The kiss was so much better than before as her taut breasts pressed against Clint. One hand left her hair and swept down pressing her closer.

"Harder." She dragged the diamond hard pebbles of her nipples against his chest, reveling in the sensation. She worked one of her hands between them and caressed his abdomen, inching closer to the waist of his sweatpants. The world spun as she found herself on her back staring up into a face carved in granite.

"Clint?"

"My turn."

Thank God she turned on the light. He wanted to turn her over. He felt the raised edges of the scars on her back. He wanted to kiss every one of them, but he was afraid it would ruin the mood. Later, when they had all night, he was going to spend hours worshiping every inch of her body. But right now was about her pleasure. He felt the fine tremors going through her body, and as much as he would like to believe it was because of their kiss, he felt the fine sheen of perspiration and knew she was spent. The woman needed another twelve hours of sleep.

"Clint, did I do something wrong?"

"Fuck no! You did everything right. You're *doing* everything right. *Too* right." He pulled at a lock of hair that had gotten caught on her lip and tucked it behind her ear.

"Before you make me lose complete control, I want to savor you." An expression of vulnerability crossed her face.

"What? Tell me."

"Don't you want me to *do* something? I need to pleasure you. I don't want you to be bored."

What kind of men had she been with?

"Baby, with you in my bed there's no chance of me ever being bored. You tempt me beyond bearing, and I want to enjoy you. Your job is to let me know if I'm doing anything wrong."

She clutched his shoulders like they were a lifeline. He grasped her hands and kissed them, and then he spread her arms wide. He caressed her arms with the backs of his hands until she arched upwards and sighed.

"Can you keep your hands there?"

"But then I won't be able to touch you."

"That's the idea. You get to touch next time, I promise." She bit her plump bottom lip, the rose color turning white. He pulled it away from her teeth and watched fascinated as the blood rushed back turning it an even darker red. He swept in for another kiss.

God, she went to his head like the headiest tequila. She flowered open for him, and he tasted the warmth and flavor that was uniquely Lydia. She whimpered and he broke away so he could trail biting kisses down her neck. Her beautiful caramel skin called to him like a siren's song. He was breaking into a sweat trying not to rush his way to the beauty of her breasts.

"Please." It was all she had to say and he found himself licking around her nipple, his hands molding her firm flesh. He looked up at her face from hooded eyes.

"More Clint, I need more. Please, don't make me beg."

"Never Lydia."

His lips surrounded the tip of her breast and laved the pebbled flesh while he gently plucked the other nipple. She moaned her pleasure, arching upwards into his caresses. She responded beautifully. He ached. It was going to kill him not to take her tonight. He never had a woman mirror his needs so exactly.

Long minutes he savored this woman. It was so much more than just her lush body and beautiful soul; it was the miracle of having this woman alive when she could have been so easily taken from him. It took everything he had not to grab and clutch and ensure she was real and in his arms.

Lydia moaned as she undulated beneath him, for just a moment he worried he had been too rough, but then above the roaring in his ears he heard her words.

"So good. So good."

He continued to caress her breasts as he trailed kisses down her sternum, licking his way ever downwards. Her breath hitched. Finally, he had to release her, as he eased her panties off.

"Lydia?" Tracing fingers up her smooth thighs he found them closed.

"I uhm." She cupped the side of his face, and he arched into her touch. "Please Clint, let me pleasure you." He heard a hint of desperation in her voice.

"Baby, everything we've done and will do, gives me pleasure."

"Truly?"

He felt her relax and gently parted her legs.

"Having your trust pleases me." His cock pressed hungrily into the mattress at the sight of her. He skimmed the soft petals of her sex, opening her so he could torture both of them. She glistened in welcome, and he gathered up her moisture and brought it to his mouth to taste. Perfection.

He bent to her and languidly licked, soothing and then igniting with his fingers and his tongue. Lydia moaned his name, and he redoubled his efforts. Stroke after stroke he took her higher until she arched into him and sobbed in ecstasy. He moved up and embraced her trembling body. She cuddled close to him like a kitten who just found a warm blanket. As soon as he thought that, she started to purr, and he realized it was the sound of delicate snoring.

"Ah Baby. You rest." Then he gave a soft huff of laughter, thankful she hadn't been awake to hear him use the 'R' word, he didn't want anything plucked.

7

CONSIDERING HE WAS IN THE NAVY YOU'D THINK HE'D HAVE enjoyed steering a boat, but not on the interstate. At least it was mostly flat, he couldn't imagine driving this in the Rockies where he grew up.

"Why are you frowning?"

"I'm not frowning. I'm concentrating."

"Why are you concentrating so hard? It's a beautiful day."

Clint spared a quick glance for Lydia. They were on a two lane road near Tallahassee, and he was happy to see her sitting up and her color looking so good.

"It is a beautiful day, especially now my navigator is awake."

"That's a bunch of hooey, you needed a navigator as much as you needed a dress. The last time I tried to tell you which way to go, I almost had us going in the wrong direction."

He laughed. She was directionally challenged.

"But I can pour you a cup of coffee, if you'd like."

"I would love it." Clint didn't know how Finn arranged

such a fully equipped RV, but it was fantastic. There had even been coffee beans and a grinder in the galley. He really owed his team mate.

"You know, I don't know how he does it."

"Who?" Lydia continued to pour the coffee into the mug for him.

"Finn."

"What does he do?"

"Not only does he get us a vehicle in the middle of the state where we need it, but he even has the bag of coffee beans I like stocked in the galley. He's scary."

Lydia handed him his coffee. "I bet they say that about you when you find the information they need on-line." She settled back into the passenger seat and he could feel her staring at him.

"Okay, I see your point." God she had gorgeous legs.

"Have you heard from them?"

"I spoke to Dare a couple of nights ago."

"I like the men you work with. I hoped when I joined the police force I would find the same sense of unity."

"How is it you didn't notice the trouble your father got himself in to?" Damn, he felt like such an asshole asking the question, but it had been bothering him ever since he had found out what classes she took in college.

"Papa's involvement started in middle school so it was just a part of life. There were a couple of odd things I thought about when I was taking the Criminology classes, but I was trying to double major and graduate early, so I laughed it off. I figured it was just my over-active imagination. I was *so* stupid."

"Not stupid, just a normal kid. We always believe the best out of our parents."

"I can't believe I wore blinders like I did. I feel like I

was a partner to his crimes."

"You can't feel that way, Lydia. If you'd really suspected something and turned a blind eye, then you would have a reason to feel guilty." He glanced at her and saw she was considering his words.

"Hey, look at the sign. It looks like we finally found the perfect greasy spoon." Clint took the exit and grinned. He parked next to a big rig truck in no time. He loved the name of the place, Tal-A-See-It-Burgers.

Lydia turned quite a few heads as they made their way in. The yellow sun dress set off her warm brown skin, and the fall of black curls down her back made her look like a beauty queen. Clint put his arm around her as they were guided to a booth near the window.

The waitress put the menus and napkin wrapped silverware in front of them. Lydia immediately unwrapped hers and looked at the spoon. She gave him an arch look.

"Okay, okay, I don't even know where the saying comes from. But when Mom and Dad would pack up my sister, brother and I on a road trip they would always look for some diner. The trick was to find one where there were a lot of truckers, because they would know where to find the good food. Dad used to call them 'greasy spoons'. Even more of a score is if they had a cool name. So this should be great!"

"I'm sold because the utensils are clean." They looked up as the waitress came over and brought them glasses of water.

"I'll be right back to take your orders."

Clint grinned when he saw breakfast was served all day. They left the hotel in Georgia at noon. Lydia slept in, and Clint enjoyed the morning just holding her. They ate some muffins and bananas stashed in the RV, but he was ready for a heaping plate of food. He'd love to see Lydia really eat a full meal as well.

When the waitress came back he ordered the steak and eggs.

"Do grits come with that?"

"You bet they do, handsome."

"I'd love a side of buttermilk pancakes as well." The waitress grinned as she wrote down his order, then she turned to Lydia.

"Now don't disappoint me and say you just want fruit and coffee."

Lydia laughed. "Oh no, I believe in eating. I want your pecan waffles and some bacon. But please don't hold it against me if I don't finish."

"You'll get points for trying. Coffee and orange juice?"

"I'd love some milk too," Lydia said as she handed the woman her menu.

"Coming right up."

The food came hot and fresh and fast. Clint lost the fight over the maple syrup.

"Mine." Lydia said as she poured it over her waffles. "You've got a mountain of food, and you can just wait to drown your pancakes." He laughed. He did it a lot around her.

"What's that?"

"Grits." He plopped on an extra tab of butter and stirred. Then scooped up a forkful and found himself a mouthful of heaven. He almost choked and grabbed his glass of water.

"Are you all right?"

"I'm fine," he assured her.

"It's the mush isn't it? It tastes like wallpaper paste and it choked you." Her brown eyes sparkled with mirth.

"Actually missy, I was thinking to myself I just found a mouthful of heaven, and then I remembered the other night when my mouth was filled with something much better."

"Clint Archer you just be quiet." She looked over her shoulder to make sure nobody was listening in on their conversation, and he laughed out loud. Teasing Lydia Hidalgo was pure joy.

"How was your conversation last night with your parents?"

"Mama actually sounded kind of relieved. I think having us all together has been stressful for her."

Clint cut into his steak. It was cooked perfectly. "How was it stressful?"

"She was trying to be all things to all of us." She hesitated and looked at him. "Can I be really honest?"

"I wish you would."

"I'm mad at her too. I try not to show it, but she's my mother, she can feel it." Clint put down his knife and fork and grabbed her hand.

"Tell me about it."

"She had to have known some of what was going on. I'm so mad at her, and I'm so disappointed in both of them." She squeezed his hand hard and he let her.

"It's understandable."

"Do you know what almost happened to Beth? Do you? How dare they?" She covered her mouth and looked around the restaurant. Nobody was looking at them.

"Let it out Lydia."

"No. I've said enough." She sighed. "Anyway, that's

why I think it's easier that I'm not around. Now she only has Papa to care for she is more relaxed."

Clint did everything in his power to keep his countenance relaxed, but he wanted to beat the shit out of both of Lydia's parents. Yeah he felt bad for Beth, but when he thought about what Lydia had gone through he was ready to kill. Finally, he was ready to talk in a calm manner.

"How are your waffles?"

"I've never had pecan waffles before. These are fantastic."

"Didn't you talk to Beth too?"

"Yeah. She said the ranch was nice. She met Jack's mother. She's nice. I think she's nervous around his step-father and step-brother."

"How about Jack? Is she nervous around him?"

"No, she sounded like she was beginning to trust him a little. I was surprised."

He watched as she swirled her bacon in the syrup and took a bite. It was so sexy the way she relished her food. Then she took a sip of milk, and was left with a trace of liquid on her upper lip. As she talked about her sister, all he could do was think about licking her lips, kissing her, sucking her tongue into his mouth.

"Don't you think so?"

"What?" Clint shifted in his seat and looked down at his cold eggs. Damn, he hoped they didn't have to walk out of here soon, he needed a few minutes to calm down. The waitress came over to top off the coffee.

"I'd ask if you if you didn't like your food, but I think I know what the problem was, hun." She gave Clint a wink and walked off.

"What's she talking about?" Lydia asked.

"Our waitress figured out I was too busy staring at you to finish eating breakfast."

Lydia looked down at Clint's plate that was only halfway eaten and eyed him.

"You ordered too much food."

"Baby, this is an appetizer. Give me your hand." Lydia thrust out her arm, palm up and Clint grasped it between both of his. "Even though we're going to make it to Tampa tonight and we could start staying at the safe house, I made reservations at a hotel overlooking the Bay."

"You did?"

"I did. I thought you might like to have dinner on the balcony of our room and watch the water."

She gave him a slow smile. "I would love that."

Yep, he was definitely walking out of the diner with a hard-on.

IT SHOULDN'T MATTER. It really shouldn't matter. But it did. Lydia looked down into her suitcase and saw two more clean sleep shirts. More clean boring underwear. Another pair of clean jeans and a clean sweater, and the one really cute thing she had to wear, she was wearing!

She'd been hiding out in the bathroom for damn near an hour. Clint had to know something was up, but every time he knocked, she said she'd be out in 'just a minute'.

She swiped at her eyes. Dammit. There's no crying in football. Soccer. Whatever the fuck they called fucking FUTball in this country. Or was it baseball? She slammed her suitcase down onto the closed lid of the toilet.

"Lydia?"

"What?" she yelled. Then she winced. She didn't want

Clint to know he had been cuddling an irrational woman for the last three nights. Damn this recovery! But she *wasn't* crazy. This *was* a big deal. She wanted to look really pretty. She wanted to wear something nice.

She took a big breath. What was it her friend from Memphis used to say? *Suck it up, Buttercup.* She looked in the mirror. Her hair and teeth were brushed. Her makeup was fresh. It was as good as it was going to get. Oh yeah, she needed to smile. She repaired the little bit of mascara that smeared from her runaway tear and opened the bathroom door, and found herself staring into the green fleece of Clint's sweatshirt. His arm was leaning against the bathroom doorframe.

She bent back her neck and saw the concerned look on his face.

"You doing better, Baby?"

She worked hard to keep on the smile she had perfected in front of the mirror. "I'm fine. I'm sorry I worried you."

"Not worried, just a little concerned. Sounded like you were ref'ing a game in there."

"What?"

He tucked one unruly curl behind her ear. "You were talking about football and soccer and then baseball. I thought you might be trading me in for a professional athlete or something."

Shit, did she say that out loud?

"Come with me. There's something I want to do before dinner." He ran his hand down her bare arm exposed by the yellow cotton sundress. He ushered her out of the room and into the hallway towards the elevator.

When they stepped onto the elevator, she looked around the six people with her, and told herself to get a grip. Yeah, there might be an outrageously dressed couple, but there was also a tired mother and father who obviously just been to the beach with their two little children. So she wasn't totally out of place. Still…

Clint guided her out the elevator, through the lobby then outside to the promenade of shops that connected the hotel to three others. Twinkling lights dotted all the little potted palm trees, and people from all walks of life were peering in windows of the different stores.

The first one that caught Lydia's eyes had crystal geodes. Holding the door open was a rock almost as tall as the two little boys who were crouched down in front of it. They were clearly fascinated with the purple amethyst crystal shattered across the inside, making it sparkle and glow.

"Dad, do all rocks look like this inside?" One of the boys asked the tall man standing next to him.

Lydia and Clint watched him give a relieved look when the clerk came over to explain about agates and geodes to the boys.

"So what did you want to do before dinner?" Lydia was relaxing now in the warm Florida air. It didn't hurt that Clint was holding her hand and looking at her like she hung the moon.

"I thought we might look around in there." He nodded at a woman's boutique coming up on the left. It looked fun and flirty, just the type of place she would normally shop if she was still home in Mexico City. But there she had a part time job at a computer store repairing old motherboards, so she could afford things not covered by her scholarship. Here in the United States she was broke.

"I think I just want to go back up to the room. I'm getting hungry."

Clint looked around the walkway, and found an empty bench under a tree and pulled her over to it. Before she sat down, he brushed off the fallen leaves. She loved how considerate he was.

"Lydia, I'm more of the blunt type. I'm really not all that good at subterfuge. We have others on the team for that." He wasn't looking at her; he was looking at the hem of her dress. This couldn't be good.

"Just tell me."

"I called my sister, Jenny. Drake is out of town, and he's the one I talk to when I need help understanding women. I mean women who matter."

"Drake?" Lydia asked in an incredulous tone.

"Sure. He really understands women."

"Drake Avery? The guy who's even bigger than you who doesn't know when to shut up? The one who's constantly bossing Beth around in the jungle?" Clint was finally looking at her and he looked indignant.

"Yes, that Drake. Look, he says stupid shit, I get that. But he has three sisters. He loves them to distraction. He really understands the female mind."

Lydia choked and gripped Clint's bicep, she started laughing softly, and then it built until it was a full-fledged belly laugh.

"Hey."

"You can't really believe that Clint. Tell me you don't really believe that. Please tell me you're smarter than that."

"He loves them."

"I'm sure he does." She dipped her head and let it drop onto his shoulder, feeling better than she had since they left their bed that morning. Then she stiffened and looked up at him.

"Wait just a damn minute. You've been reading me right, and we've been communicating fine for months. Clint, you've been the nerd-king to my dork-queen."

"Until today. Today you lost your shit, and it wasn't from being sick. I heard you in the bathroom. I heard how mad and sad you were and it scared the piss out of me."

"So you wanted to call Drake, instead of talking to me, but had to settle for your sister?" Lydia tried to keep her tone calm and rational. She looked around to make sure no one could hear them, but everyone was oblivious to their conversation.

"Come here, Baby," he opened his arms, and she gladly snuggled against him. He cupped her head and tucked it beneath his chin.

"I'm sorry, I didn't do any of this to make you feel bad. I was trying to make you feel *happy*. I knew I needed some advice."

Just listening to the beat of his heart helped her calm down and listen to his words. Finally, he asked. "Is this a clothes thing? A money thing?"

She gulped. Tears once again stinging her eyes. She pressed her face harder against his neck. "So stupid. Someone tried to *kill* me. My father tried to *kill* himself. I don't even know *where* my sister is. I'm such a spoiled brat. But I wanted to look pretty for you." *Oh God, here came the tears.*

"Did you ever think it's exactly because of those things that trying to get control of some little aspect of your life matters? Lydia, you haven't been in charge of shit since they kidnapped you." She absorbed his words and he was right.

"There's two ways we can go about this." He stroked his hand from the top of her head down to the curve of her waist, again and again. She softened against him, no longer caring who was watching.

"What are my choices?" She was hoping one of them included going back up to the room and skipping food. They had yet to make real love, and that's what she wanted. Clint kept insisting she 'rest'. And dammit considering how fast she fell asleep each night apparently he was right.

"What did you ask?" His breath tickled her ear.

"I asked what my choices were."

"One, I give you my credit card and you go into the shop and buy whatever the hell your heart desires. Lucky for you I happen to have a very high limit with an excellent credit rating." She giggled.

"It sounds like you're trying to sell yourself to me."

"Fuck yeah. I want you to know I'm a good bet."

"Okay, that was option number one, what's number two?"

"You fulfill a fantasy I have ever since I got off the phone with Jenny. I go into a shop with you, and you go into a dressing room and come out modelling outfit after outfit, making me so hard that by the time we get to the room we'll have to eat dinner for breakfast."

Clint's heartbeat was no longer the slow and easy rhythm it had been, it sped up to match hers. She prayed they had lingerie at the shop and a discreet salesperson.

CLINT CARRIED the two shopping bags in one hand, and kept his other hand securely around Lydia. She damn near killed him at the boutique and it was wonderful. He saw a flirtatious side to her that was new. He expected this is how it would have been if they met in Mexico City.

The girl had moves! When she came out in a little red number, he damn near swallowed is tongue. The clerk found some sexy red heels to go with the dress, and the skirt hit her mid-thigh. Lydia explained this was a clubbing outfit. Clint wasn't sure about her ever going out in public in the outfit, as least not without him there to warn off the riff-raff, but he loved seeing her eyes light up.

"I just couldn't resist trying it on. This is not one I want to buy, this was a 'torture Clint dress'," she explained.

"It worked," he said hoarsely. "It goes into the 'buy' pile." She twisted and grabbed the price tag.

"Oh hell no. But I'm glad to see it worked." She gave him a wicked smile and closed the curtain of the dressing room. He called over the salesperson.

"Jessica, can you make sure to wrap that up where Lydia can't see it?"

"You've got it." She winked at him. "The shoes too?"

"Of course."

When he opened the door to their room, the scent of food hit them immediately. She looked at him curiously. His hand slid over the blue silk of her top that went with her new Capri pants.

"I called the hotel and arranged for dinner to be sent up while Jessica was ringing us up."

Lydia went over to the balcony and saw there was a bottle of champagne chilling as well. "Just how much do Navy SEALS make?"

"I'm a saver. I rent a two-bedroom apartment that isn't much. Sometimes I do side computer consulting work. Want to see my bank statements?"

"If I do, I won't have to ask, I'll just hack into your

bank." He laughed as she lifted one of the lids from an entrée. "Geez Clint, how much food did you order?"

"I eat a lot. I wasn't sure what you would like, so I ordered a variety. Trust me, whatever you don't eat, I will." He moved behind her, and tucked the fall of her hair over her left shoulder so he could kiss the right side of her neck. She shuddered.

She turned and slid her arms around his waist. "Keep doing that and we won't eat."

"Food first, we're going to need our strength for what I have planned." He pulled out the chair for her to sit down. He watched as she crossed her legs and he saw her painted toes in her new sandals.

Picking up her plate, he asked her what she wanted. He served her bruschetta, stuffed mushrooms, a piece of salmon, a couple of beef medallions and some potatoes.

"Clint, I'm holding you to your promise that you'll finish what I can't eat," Lydia said as she started in on her meal. "I just wanted to taste everything, but there is no way I'll finish all of this."

"Trust me, I'll make sure everything gets taken care of." He poured some champagne and sat back in his chair. He couldn't ever remember having had such a romantic night with a woman before. She was glowing, he had wanted to spoil her, to make her feel cherished, and seeing her look of delight convinced him he had succeeded. It was a heady experience.

"I want my dessert now." Her voice felt like velvet across his skin. When he put his hand on the lid that covered the chocolate torte, she covered it with hers.

"That's not the dessert I want. I want something a lot richer and decadent than mere chocolate."

"Thank fuck." He pushed back his chair and it started

to tip over, but he grabbed it before it fell. "Damn woman, you go to my head."

She stood up a hell of a lot more gracefully than he had. She moved like a dancer. He imagined her dancing in that red dress and all the blood in his body rushed south of his belt buckle. He stood staring at her.

"Clint?"

He picked her up, cradling her like he wanted in the jungle, with one arm around her back, and his other under her knees. She fit him perfectly, and he wasn't hurting her. She sighed and smiled.

"I love your strength. It saved me." He walked taller as he moved them inside. He laid her down on the white down comforter of the king sized bed.

"Lydia, your strength has amazed me from the moment we met." He looked at her carefully, and saw a hint of vulnerability beneath the excitement.

"We're not going to do anything you don't want to do tonight, you know that, don't you, Baby?"

"I want everything." She wiggled into a sitting position and unbuttoned the top button of his shirt, then the second, and the third. She splayed her hand inside, teasing his chest hair. "I love how warm you are."

He stayed still as she finished unbuttoning his shirt, and then she nuzzled her cheek against his chest, breathing in deeply.

He grabbed a handful of her silky hair and brought it to his face and inhaled. The scent went straight to his cock. Everything about her was so intensely feminine. His hand brushed the zipper at the back of her top and he lowered it. He couldn't wait to see which bra she was wearing. Lydia stiffened in his arms. He felt the scars.

"Shhh, I saw them the other night."

"I–I know." He thought it through. She'd been so tired. He'd been giving comfort as much as making love. Tonight was different.

"What do you need?" Was she going to be shy? Did she need the light off tonight? He'd do whatever this woman needed.

"It's pretty ugly." She was looking down at her hands resting on his chest. He tipped up her chin so she couldn't fail to see and hear him.

"Every one of those scars is a badge of honor. The only reason it will bother me to see them is to think if we'd only gotten there sooner we could have saved you the torture."

"No! You can't think that way." Lydia cupped his face, and placed a tender kiss on his lips. "You saved me. The beating is on them."

Brown eyes met hazel. "If I can begin to forgive myself, can you believe me when I tell you I see only beauty?" She finally nodded, and his eyes lightened, and laugh lines fanned from the edges.

"Ever since you bought those three bras, I've been dying to know which one you decided to wear tonight." He pulled the top over her head.

"Ah Ha. You wore the silver one." She laughed at his silliness. But then his expression turned carnal.

"Look at your nipples. I can see them through the lace. You're gorgeous. You're going to kill me tonight." He tangled the fingers of one hand in the curls of her hair as he took her mouth in a voracious kiss. His tongue plundered, as his other hand found the latch on the back of her bra and released the bounty. He lowered her slowly against the pillows, barely able to think as she met his passion. The prick of her fingernails in his scalp only added to the spice of the kiss.

Their bodies were in perfect accord. She spread her legs in welcome, and he was now resting against her, while she rocked upwards.

"This feels so perfect, please. Please now."

"Soon. I promise, soon. But first I want to explore you. I want to cherish every moment of our time tonight."

Clint slid her bra totally off her body, and then swept downwards so her slacks and panties followed. He lowered his head toward her breast and she shoved against him. Hard.

"What?"

"We did this before and I don't want a repeat."

"Huh?"

"I missed out." He was totally confused. All he understood was she was looking at him with a really serious look, and he better get his head in the game if he wanted to get close to Lydia. Then she stroked her hands downwards to the button at the top of his jeans.

"I didn't get equal playing time last time," she said as she started to unbutton the top button of his jeans. Feeling her hand as it brushed against his lower abdomen made him lose all focus. He got up off the bed.

"Clint," she whined.

"If you help me out of my jeans, this will be over too fucking fast. Your hands that close to my cock will drive me out of my mind."

"That's the idea." She rubbed her legs together, and her hands moved upwards towards her breasts and cupped them. Holy hell!

"You stop that right now Lydia Hidalgo. We're taking this slow. You just got out of the hospital five days ago."

"Exactly. I deserve my treat now. Fast first. Slow second." She moved one of her hands towards her face, and brought her forefinger to her lips and sucked it. He shoved his jeans down. Where the fuck was the condom?

CLINT DESTROYED her three nights ago. She had never been loved so thoroughly before. It never even occurred to her a man would give and not expect something in return. She wanted to give him the same kind of pleasure tonight. She wanted to be the type of woman men fantasized about, something she never managed to be for others, but a woman she knew she could be for Clint. She wanted to make all of his dreams come true.

Lydia pulled her wet finger out of her mouth, and trailed it down her neck to the upper part of her breast, loving how Clint's eyes narrowed and followed her every move. Slowly she swirled it around her areola. As his eyes focused on her breasts, she glanced downwards and saw how hard and erect he was. Her thighs clenched together as warmth pooled. The idea of having that much power inside of her was arousing and...intimidating. She sucked in a deep breath.

Clint's gaze cut upwards, and he was on the bed beside her before she could exhale.

"Talk to me, Baby."

She lifted her breasts in offering, wanting to focus his attention back towards her body, not her nervous reactions.

He stroked the tops of her breasts with his calloused fingertips, dragging them across her sensitive flesh. Her hands fell to her sides, as the world narrowed to the shards of pleasure his touch evoked.

"Talk to me, what were you thinking a minute ago?" She came out of her pleasure induced trance, and rolled to her side. Tonight was about Clint. Looking at him and his body she had to touch.

"Want this. Need this." She stroked down his rock hard abdomen and grasped his cock. So hot, so hard. "I need you, Clint."

"We'll get there." He placed a soft kiss against her temple.

She grazed her thumb over the silky head of his penis and gloried when she felt him shudder. She raised her knee. "Now."

"You're amazing. But you're not going to make me lose my head." He kissed the corner of her mouth, and she felt his strained smile. "You, lady, need to be with me every step of the way."

"But I want what you want." She finally had to look away from Clint's steady gray gaze.

"This is about both of us, love, which means you're going to talk to me." She gave him another stroke and he arched into her hand. He put his hand over hers and looked her in the eye.

"Lydia?"

"I'm not sure I'm ready for you." She gave him a squeeze and looked up at him, praying he would understand. He searched her eyes and seemed to find an answer to his question.

"It's my job to make sure you are. Do you trust me?"

"More than anybody else in my life. You would never let me down."

He nodded, then he stroked down her body, and pushed out her raised knee, so that he could touch the intimate flesh of her core.

"You feel like wet silk." He pushed a finger inside and she sighed in pleasure. Two, and she moaned as he made her feel so good. But when he tried to increase his presence even more, she winced.

His eyes narrowed. "We're going to slow down, Baby."

"No. I want more *now*." She didn't care it was uncomfortable. She needed to give to him this time.

He chuckled at her petulant tone. "This is too important. You're too important." He pulled her hand away from his flesh, and brought it to his mouth for a kiss. "Your touch is potent, Lady."

Lydia smiled, and stroked the muscles of his back as he pressed teasing kisses down her body. She might have wanted to make this all about Clint tonight, but her greedy body took the choice away from her.

"Ahhh. Clint."

His tongue swirled down her tummy, and then he was exactly where she wanted him. He parted her folds and when she tried to rise to his tongue's forays, his grip held her down, which rocketed her arousal upwards. He delved deep as his thumb raised the hood of her clit, and then he sucked as he plunged his fingers deep finding just the right spot. She moaned her release.

As she crested he found heaven. This woman meant the world to him and no matter his needs hers would always come first. He continued to plumb her depths, swirling his tongue over her engorged flesh.

"No more, I can't." And then she did. This time she cried out.

He sheathed himself and slowly entered her hot depths.

"So good, you feel so good, Clint." Her nails bit into his back. Resting one arm over her head, he smoothed her hair from her mouth, and kissed her lips, as he eased in further. He read only pleasure on her face as she canted upwards, and then he felt her body give a pulse of wet welcome. He started a gentle tempo she matched, but soon she shoved against him in eager awkward thrusts.

His hand slid down her hip and guided her. Soon they were meeting one another in a rhythm that launched them ever upwards.

"Please." She shuddered.

He hit the spot, the one he touched before with his fingers, in and out. She clamped down on him and they came together in a shower of ecstasy.

Lydia looked at him with a dreamy expression, and he knew he was wearing a silly grin on his face.

"Don't move a muscle." He went to the bathroom. He got back in time to see her stretch her body and he groaned.

She curled around one of the pillows and looked at him.

"I've never felt better in my life."

He walked around the bed and got in behind her. She stiffened, but stayed where she was. He laid a kiss on her shoulder and started tracing the ridges of her scars.

"Do they hurt?"

"Sometimes they do," she said quietly, "not recently."

His breath shuddered in. He'd known what to expect. He'd asked Darius. But knowing and seeing were two different things. She rolled over, exposing the entire expanse of her back to him.

"Baby, you should have told me, you should never have been lying on your back when we made love."

"Clint, I only felt your touch." He brushed kisses and traced the network of marks that marred her skin. He wasn't surprised when he tasted the salt of his tears.

Lydia fell asleep and he pulled her close covering them up with the comforter.

"I love you, baby. You're mine."

8

THEY MADE IT TO THE SAFE HOUSE A COUPLE OF HOURS AGO. Finn arranged for a three bedroom, two story house a mile from the beach. Clint thought it was perfect because it was at the end of a cul-de-sac.

Lydia pressed end on the phone and turned to Clint.

"Beth learned how to ride a horse!"

Clint looked at Lydia's beaming face, momentarily diverted from his computer screen. *Score one for Jack Preston.*

"So Mama Bear is feeling a little bit better?" Clint teased.

"Yes I am."

Lydia got up from the dining room table as the buzzer rang in the kitchen. She took out the casserole she put in for dinner.

"So that takes care of Beth, but you didn't tell me how your conversation with your parents went."

Clint closed his laptop. He wanted to show Lydia what he found on Guzman, but he could tell she needed to talk.

"I honestly don't know what to think." She looked at

him, and then touched the glass dish without using the oven mitt.

"Ow."

In seconds he had her hand under the faucet, running cold water on the burn.

"It's no big deal. Really." He kissed the top of her head.

"Let me take care of you. I like doing it, okay?"

She leaned into him. "Don't tell anyone, but I kind of like it when you take care of me too." Now didn't that deserve another kiss? He continued to keep her hand under the water, but he used his other to tangle in her mass of black curls and tip her head for a fierce kiss that left them both breathless.

Reluctantly he let her go.

"Is there anything you want to talk about?"

"Not really. They're just them. In five more weeks, this will all be over."

She straightened. "Help me find where the plates are."

They scrounged in the cupboards and found the dishes they needed to set the table. "This is a really nice house. Do you know who it belongs to?" Lydia asked as they sat down.

"Nope. Finn arranged it. The man is amazing. He has contacts everywhere. You mention you need something, and voila, it just shows up."

"Does he use computers too?"

"I'm sure he does but it's not like we do. It's more just e-mailing a bunch of friends and calling in favors." Clint laughed.

He waited for her to pick up her fork. Then he did the same, anxious to try the food that had been tantalizing him for the last half hour while it cooked. He took a bite of the succulent corn and chicken dish and sighed with delight.

"I love this."

"I'm glad you like it."

"How's your hand?" She seemed to be holding her fork okay.

"Fine. So what did you find out while I was talking to Beth?" she asked as she took another delicate bite of her food. Damn, she was sexy when she ate. Okay, he admitted to himself, she was sexy when she did anything as far as he was concerned.

"I've been accessing the dark web."

"Makes sense. That's where most of the information about drug trafficking goes on."

"Something weird is going on. I wanted you to take a look at it. Guzman seems to be dumping his product at a fast rate. Almost like he is having a fire sale. It doesn't make any sense to me."

"Hmmm." Lydia put down her fork after only a few small bites.

"Nope, you have to finish a hell of a lot more before you get to play with my computer." She gave him a dark look.

"I have my own damn computer."

"Yeah, but it would take you an hour to get to the site I found. If you're a good girl and eat all your food, you could be looking at the fun stuff in under twenty minutes." She stuck out her tongue at him.

He choked out a laugh and her eyes twinkled.

"You're perfect for me, you know that, don't you?" She blushed and picked up her fork.

"I'm serious. When we get done with this shit, I want to take you to Colorado to meet my family."

She took a slow bite of her food and swallowed. "Tell me about them. Your family I mean."

"It's pretty normal. Mom, Dad, my sister Jenny and my brother Robert. They all still live in Denver."

He watched as she started to push food around on her plate.

"Baby, what's wrong?"

"Nothing." God, he hated that answer.

"Lydia, please talk to me."

"Normal sounds so good. You're lucky." She set down her fork and took her plate to the sink. Dammit, she had barely eaten. She started cleaning up the kitchen while he finished the rest of his meal. She looked so sad. How had they gone from her joking with him, to this?

He went into the kitchen with his dishes and put them in the dishwasher. She avoided looking at him. He couldn't stand it a second longer. He trapped her against the edge of the counter.

"Clint, what are you doing?"

"Trying to determine what made you sad."

"Nothing." That damn word again.

He put his hand on her forehead.

"No fever."

She knocked his hand away. "You're being silly."

"You're not being honest with me." She looked up at him with confused brown eyes.

"I'm not trying to be dishonest." He saw only truth.

"Baby, tell me what you're feeling. I hate when you shut me out." He did. He hated it a lot.

"Normal. You called your family normal." She almost spit out the word. Now he was wearing a confused expression.

"The Hidalgos are never going to be normal again. You

need to run away from me Clint. I'm trouble." He pressed her against the cupboards.

"There isn't a chance in hell I'm going to run. And, there is no way I'm going to let you run. I have no idea where this is leading, but we are going to find out." She twisted, trying to get away from him, but he was more than happy to use his strength to keep her in his arms.

"Are you listening to me?"

"Are you listening to me, Clint? We're on the run from one of the most notorious drug cartels in the world. My father worked for that drug cartel. We will all have to go into the Witness Protection Program. We left normal three Twilight Zone episodes ago." She shoved at his shoulders. "Let me go."

"No."

"Are you threatening me?" If he had seen the slightest bit of fear on her beloved features he would have let her go, but he saw only anger and frustration.

"I'm not threatening you, I'm telling you that you don't get to leave this discussion until you bring up some sort of rational argument."

"You are a horse's ass! You need to get the hell away from me. You have a normal happy family. You are one of your country's heroes. The last thing you need is someone like me in your life."

"That's it. You've officially gone off the rails." His hands tenderly framed her face, and he used his thumb to rescue her bottom lip from her teeth. She grasped his biceps and her lower body softened, providing him a cradle to lean into.

Her breath caressed his lips as he dipped in to taste. He could feel her conflict, and he wasn't going to allow it. He thrust his tongue deep and she gasped, arching into him. He moved, one arm tilting her up, the other lifting her up, so she was seated on the granite countertop. She pushed him away with one arm, and pulled him closer with the other. This was not going to be how they would spend their time together.

He pulled her right leg around his waist, so even through their layers of clothes they could feel each other's heat. She relaxed and stopped trying to push him away.

Clint drifted kisses down the side of her neck, loving how she always smelled of honeysuckle.

"This won't change anything. We're still wrong for one another." Her fingers dug deeply into his scalp. He loved it.

"Nobody else will put up with Nerd King." She gripped his hair and pulled him away. Tears were swimming in her big brown eyes.

"I'm serious."

"So am I. I'm the furthest thing away from normal you could imagine. I need you. Please just keep yourself open to the possibility." She gave him a look so filled with hope and fear he had to trace her lips with kisses.

"And another thing." He tipped up her chin so she was looking him in the eye.

"What?"

"When I ask you what's wrong, I'm begging you. I'll get down on my knees if I have to. Please don't say 'nothing'. That answer just scares the piss out of me."

She giggle snorted. "Hand me a paper towel you fool." Lydia blew her nose. "So now do we get to play on the computers?"

"HOW OLD WERE you when you started playing with computers?" Lydia asked. They were sitting cross legged on the floor in front of the coffee table in the den. Each of them were in front of their respective laptops. They spent a half hour arguing over the better operating systems, the better hardware, and game controllers. Now they were settling into the business of investigation. Clint liked to call it spying.

"I took apart my first motherboard when I was nine. What about you?"

"Eight." She smirked. She glanced over at his screen and he angled his computer so she couldn't see it.

"No cheating off of my paper."

Lydia fought down a yawn but Clint saw it. He got up and left the room. He was soon back with pillows from a bed, and a plate of cheese, crackers, and fruit.

"Stand up." Lydia didn't even bother to ask why, she just stood. He pushed the table closer to the couch, then positioned the pillows so she could sit on them and rest against them while still working with her laptop. He helped her to sit back down.

"You hardly ate anything at dinner so you need to eat this. If you don't, I'm going to say no more computer games for you tonight." Lydia reached for a cube of cheese and saw the slight trembling in her hand. Clint didn't say a word, he just got up and left the room. Damn, she knew he had seen that.

"Here's a full glass of water, and another one of grape juice. You have to finish both of these as well."

Part of her wanted to give him a bitchy comment, but he was right. She'd be all up in Beth's business if she wasn't taking care of herself. She leaned against the pillows and sipped the beverages and ate the food.

"So you were a computer prodigy but still feel the need to cheat off my work?"

"You're the one who calls this *spying*." She grinned. "I wouldn't be doing my job if I didn't look at all the angles and information available to me."

"So you cheated in school?"

Her hand jerked involuntarily as she was bringing the grape juice to her lips. Liquid spilled down the front of her white top. "Of course not! Cheating in school is wrong." She saw Clint laughing at her.

"You sure are fun to tease." He popped a cracker into his mouth.

"You're an ass." She grabbed the last cracker before he could get it.

"Okay, so when did you start your investigation on Guzman."

"It's really kind of weird. I was already investigating his organization before I knew Papa ever worked for him. It must have been serendipity."

"Why were you investigating him?"

"It was part of my criminology course. Me and two classmates decided we could impress our professor if we did a paper on an active investigation. Manuel's uncle worked for the coroner's office so he got some information on a hit done in the Tepito neighborhood. It was perfect because my family used to live there when I was in grade school, so I still had friends there."

"Isn't that a high crime area?"

"Yes." She looked at Clint, but didn't see any judgment on his face.

"Mason's fiancé, Sophia, had some problems in a bad part of San Diego. Her little brother ran away, and she was out looking for him in the middle of the night. She still does volunteer work in a mission down there, and he always worries when she's there and he can't be with her."

"Many good people live in high crime areas, but they live good productive lives. Sometimes they also need help. I think it's wonderful Sophia volunteers some of her time at this mission."

"Did you ever run into problems there?"

She tried to push up from the pillows, but her hand hit the floor instead and she hissed in a breath.

"Are you okay?"

"It's nothing." Her head jerked up. "I mean I hit my hand in the same place I burned it. Look I need to go to the bathroom. I'll be right back." Clint lent her a hand up, and she damn near raced out of the room.

She knew she was staying in the bathroom too long, but she really didn't want to go out there again. Her hands trembled as she wet a towel and wiped the cool cloth over her face. Clint knocked on the door.

She looked at herself in the mirror. She looked like hell. Dark circles under her eyes. Her black hair looked lifeless. Too her horror she saw tears. She squeezed her eyes shut, and then opened them. Good. They were gone.

"Lydia. Are you okay?"

She opened the door. She walked to him, and wrapped her arms around his waist and he just pulled her in.

"I've got you girl. You're safe." The world shifted, and he was carrying her down the hall.

He put his knee on the bed to lay her down and she shook her head.

"No. I want to get undressed."

HE SLID her down his body. Clint had no idea what triggered her upset, but he planned to find out. When he was sure she was securely on her feet, he went over to her suitcase and found her Tasmanian devil sleepshirt. He came back and she was still standing exactly as he had left her—looking lost. He swiftly pulled her dress over her head and divested her of her bra.

"Here Baby, let's get you ready for bed." He helped her into the cartoon shirt and then pulled back the covers. God, she was killing him. He stripped and got in beside her and tucked her close. She was shivering.

He had never seen someone cry without shedding a tear, but she was doing it now. "Tell me about what it was like living in Tepito." Beth told him what happened, but now he needed Lydia to tell him. He needed to hear it from her as much as she needed to tell it.

"People died."

"Who?"

"My babysitter. Our babysitter. Angela. Her baby, Anicia died."

"Tell me."

"I was nine. I saw it all. Mama and Papa wouldn't let her babysit Beth and me anymore. They said it was too dangerous. I didn't know it at the time, but her husband Herman had been a witness to a crime and went to the police. One of the gangs was threatening reprisals, so Mama said Angela couldn't babysit us anymore."

"She had a baby?" That didn't jive with what Beth told him.

"She was six months pregnant. I got to feel her tummy. Her baby's name was Anicia."

"I was playing hopscotch when I saw Angela with her husband walking across the street. I had to go to the crosswalk to get to them. I saw a car drive by, and then I saw two guns pointing at them. There were so many shots fired. Angela and Herman never made any sounds, their bodies just kept bouncing and twitching with blood spattering everywhere." Lydia ground her forehead into his chest, her fist shoved against her mouth making it difficult to understand some of her words, but the anguish was clear.

"The light changed and I ran across the street. Nobody could stop me from getting to them, because I was little and I ran under their arms. I hugged Angela and begged her to wake up." Finally, Lydia started to cry. Thank God. His woman felt so delicate in his arms. She'd been so sick, and still wasn't eating much. She'd gone through so many horrors in her life. Clint loved that she came to him for solace.

"I have you."

"Please don't leave me."

"I won't." He rocked her, his hands gently stroking up and down on her back. Finally, her sobs turned to hiccups, and then he felt the soft breath of her sleep.

He waited until he was sure she was deeply asleep, and then he snuck out of bed. He went into the den and shut down her computer and cleaned up. He stretched out on the couch and booted up his laptop and found the articles on the killing in Tepito. He wondered if that might have been the impetus for Lydia's father to start working for the Guzman's. Clint would never agree with Hidalgo's choices, but he could begin to see his motives.

Clint set some online search parameters for potential activity between the Mexico and Texas border since it was the Guzman's preferred method of drug transport. He considered hacking into Lydia's computer so he could get some of her information and have more searches run through the night.

"But that would be cheating, wouldn't it Archer?" He laughed to himself. God, it had been funny to see Lydia get so bent out of shape when he had asked her if she had cheated in school. She would be the last person who would have cheated. She was such a straight shooter, it scared him. Her moral code was above reproach, and they might have to significantly bend some rules in order to get Guzman.

He picked up her laptop and spent a couple of minutes trying to remember her password. His extremely smart woman used a random alpha numeric code. He had watched her enter it. He knew he missed the last two numbers, that's why it took him a little bit of time to get into her system. When he did he smiled.

"Every time I find out more about you Lydia Hidalgo I fall a little more in love." The way she organized her system was a thing of beauty. It almost exactly mirrored his own.

"Shit!"

She was further into the dark web than he was. He couldn't believe the network of contacts she had. It took him an hour to find all of her e-mail accounts. When he did he no longer worried about her ability to bend the rules, she apparently shredded the rule book. She had multiple aliases, and she was gathering information like a hungry squirrel before winter.

He heard her coming down the hall. He kept poking through her files. When he looked up she was wearing the blanket from their bed like a little child.

"If you let me sit on your lap, I'll show you the really good stuff."

"Jesus Lydia, I don't know if my heart can stand the good stuff. Do you realize what you have on your computer? Do you realize the systems you've hacked into? The type of information you're privy to?"

"I bet you don't have it all figured out. You should let me sit on your lap." She scared him. He patted his lap and she snuggled against him. Her fingers fairly flew across the keyboard. He realized he missed some of her accounts.

"Thought you were all that and a bag of chips, did you?" She smirked at him.

Clint watched as she brought up an e-mail account she had from inside the Federal Ministerial Police Force. She set herself up as a contractor, and it allowed her to have an account with an address that mirrored all FMP employees. As a result, she could interact with them and get information they would not give to outsiders.

"Are you shitting me?" She kissed the bottom of his chin.

"I told you I was good."

"You're fucking amazing."

"So you don't hate me now? I've crossed some lines."

He took the computer out of her hands and put it on the coffee table.

"I admire the hell out of you, and I've *never* been so turned on in my life."

She got off his lap and let the blanket drop. She was naked. He damn near swallowed his tongue.

"In that case, let's go to bed and *not* sleep."

RAIN STARTED in Florida the same way it did in Mexico, all at once. There were no little raindrops to warn you the torrent was going to begin, the heavens just suddenly opened up. She was pressed against Clint's warm back, she felt his deep even breathing and realized he was still asleep. She eased away from him.

Lydia grabbed Clint's shirt to wear instead of her sleep shirt. She went to one of the other bedrooms and grabbed the comforter off the bed and laughed. *Comforter.* She'd never really thought about the word before, but they sure did comfort her. She wrapped it around her like she'd been doing since childhood, and went downstairs. Before she turned on any lights she could see it was a hell of downpour.

Walking into the kitchen she scrounged the back of a cupboard until she found the hot chocolate mix. She fixed herself a mug and then went to the large window overlooking the backyard. She sat cross legged in front of it and stared out, sipping her cocoa. She didn't hear Clint. She never did, he was as silent as a SEAL, but she felt him crouch down behind her.

"Are you okay?"

"The rain brings back a lot of memories. You know?" She opened her arms. "Wanna share my blanket and hot chocolate?"

"I'd love to."

He snuggled in beside her, and they sat there in the dark watching the rain and she leaned closer to him as the first boom of thunder sounded.

"I had nightmares for the first month after we left the jungle, every time it rained."

"I had nightmares no matter what," she said.

"Did you have one tonight?"

"God no." Lydia gave him a warm smile and set the

chocolate on the window sill. "How could I have a nightmare being in bed with you?"

"Lydia, that's a beautiful sentiment, but you don't have to always be strong for me, I'm not your family. I want you to know you can lean on me."

She straddled him so they were face to face. He immediately wrapped the blanket around her so she wasn't cold.

"Now you listen here, Clint Archer." Her voice was soft and fierce, her eyes warm and loving. "There are very few things I take for granted. The sun will come up in the morning. I will eventually eat any ice cream put in front of me. I can always depend and lean on Clint Archer."

"Yes, but will you, is the question. Or will you just put on the same game face you do for everyone else?" His big warm hands coasted up and down her back, and it felt so good.

"Clint, I've never trusted someone like I trust you. I trust you with my real feelings. I trust you can handle the real me. What finally convinced me was when you could put up with me the night we went shopping."

He huffed out a laugh. "Score one for me and American Express."

"You goof. I'm serious. I was pretty sure you could handle me, warts and all. So that's my long way of saying. I wasn't lying, I really *don't* have nightmares when I'm sleeping with you. I really *will* lean on you."

"It goes both ways. I trust you too. I will lean on you." He brought a hand up to caress her cheek, it trembled. "I love you Lydia Rose Hidalgo." The world stopped spinning. She looked into eyes bright green and shining with love.

"Are you sure? Please be sure."

He took her hand and brought it to his heart. "My love is going to last longer than the beating of my heart. It will last for eternity."

Tears she had been holding back spilled.

"I love you so much, Clint. You mean the world to me. You are a blessing from God."

They stood and he led her back to their bedroom. They talked and made love and talked for the rest of the night.

"CLINT, THIS CAN'T BE RIGHT." She protested three nights later.

He looked up from where he was chopping vegetables.

"You're going to have to be more specific."

"First, how the hell have you managed to tap into the US border agents? Then, how do you know they have stopped a shipment that was Guzman's? It could have been one of the other cartels."

She had her hair in a ponytail and was in a pair of short, shorts. She must have been beating off boys with a stick in college.

"Huh?"

"Are you even listening to what I'm saying? Pay attention, if not to me, at least be careful with the knife."

"Baby, handling knives is second nature." He scooped up all of the veggies and put them into the saucepan. "However trying to concentrate on what you're saying when you're wearing those shorts is beyond me."

She ran her hand from ankle to thigh. "These old things?"

"You're killing me. You're never allowed to wear those in public." She blushed.

"Clint. I hardly ever wore clothes that were too revealing, only when I was with my girlfriends when we went to clubs. I was always careful." He thought about the red dress and felt himself break into a sweat.

"Lydia, you must have had half of Mexico City chasing after you."

She shouted out a laugh. "You're good for my ego."

"Are you out of your mind? I'm serious as a heart attack." He covered the pan, and walked over to where she was sitting on the barstool.

"You're a knockout."

Lydia tilted her head and gave him a serious look and then smiled. "You really think that, don't you?"

He feathered a kiss against her lips, and then stepped back and looked her up and down. "Oh yeah. You're gorgeous."

"I'm pretty, but I'm certainly not gorgeous. But having the man I love think I am? Well a girl can't ask for anything better."

She was wrong. Hell, they'd just gone out to dinner last night and he'd seen the men eyeing her. But he wasn't going to argue the point. He'd just thank his lucky stars she was his.

"So what were you talking about before we got caught up in your beauty."

"You are such a goof," she said hitting his chest. "I wanted to know how you could tell the difference between who sent what drug shipments."

"The gang tattoos of the people who were caught smuggling." Clint went back to the stove and put water on to boil.

"Okay, now it makes sense. Are you sure I can't help with dinner?"

"Nope, you cooked the night before last." He liked showing her that he could cook. He wanted her to see what a life together could be like. His hand stilled as he held the pasta over the boiling water.

He looked back at Lydia where she was fiddling with her gaming headset. Yep, this was the woman he wanted to marry. She was perfect for him.

He heard the ringtone for Finn.

"It's my parents!" Lydia scrambled off the barstool and went into the den and answered the phone. It gave Clint time to think about how he was going to convince her to marry him. He knew they had a lot of immediate obstacles. Those were minor. He was worried about the major ones. Marriage was a big step, saying you loved someone was one thing, but marriage? Committing to a man who had his kind of job was an issue. It wasn't for everyone. There would be times he would have to leave and not tell her where he was going. Would she be able to cope?

"Clint, Finn wants to talk to you."

He took the phone and stirred the noodles.

"Can you talk?" he asked.

"Yeah, can you?"

Clint glanced out into the other room at Lydia, then turned on the overhead fan over the stove. "Yeah, I can talk."

"The father is doing better. I worry for Lydia's mom. Gloria internalizes things. She is so busy taking care of Ricardo she is a nervous wreck."

"Are they safe enough to leave the house? Do things?"

"That's another problem, Ricardo never wants to leave.

So Gloria is stuck inside with him. He just watches TV. I play cards with her. I talk to her. We're BFF's. There's parts of her that remind me of my mom."

"What about the US Marshall's?"

"They're really standoffish. I talked to them, and they told me it was a bad idea to get emotionally attached. I said it was a bad idea for them to be dicks. We're at an impasse." Clint laughed.

"I did manage to find her Achilles heel, she loves romances, so I found a used bookstore with a stash of really juicy stories all in Spanish. That seems to have really made her happy."

"Hmmm, I wonder if it would make Lydia happy."

"You mean she's not living a romance?"

"Asshole."

"So I've been reading through your e-mails. It looks like you're trying to bring down the Guzman organization."

"Yeah. The reason the Hidalgo's have to go into Witness Protection after Ricardo testifies is retribution from Guzman. If Guzman is no longer a threat, then they won't need to go into hiding."

"You don't want Lydia to disappear, do you?"

"Would you?"

"Nope."

"How's Beth doing? Have you heard from Jack?"

"She's doing well. She seems to be slowly coming out of her shell."

"Good."

The timer buzzed.

"Hey, I have to go, dinner's ready."

He plated the noodles and sauce and called Lydia. She set the table, and poured wine.

"My God Clint, this smells divine."

"Hopefully you'll like how it tastes too." She got up and brought a grater and a block of parmesan cheese.

"You forgot the cheese." She leaned over his shoulder. "How much would you like?" He leaned backwards into her breasts and looked up.

"Just keep grating until I say stop." She grated at least a half a cup and finally made an exasperated sound and stilled.

"I didn't tell you to stop."

"I figured you out, you just want to rub up against me."

"Yep." He lifted his shoulder so it brushed the inside of her breast. She moaned. He took the grater and cheese from her hand, and toppled her into his lap.

"The food will get cold," she protested. He kissed her, his tongue licking across the seam of her lips.

"To hell with the food, we can nuke it later."

"Need you. Want you. I can't live my life without you."

"Take me to bed."

"You're not hearing me, Baby." He stayed her hand as it crept up around his neck, and brought it to his cheek instead. "I need you in my life. Forever." She went still.

"You can't mean that."

"Clint, as soon as Papa testifies, all of us are going into the Witness Protection Program with him."

"Is that really what you want?" She melted closer and slid her fingers through the opening between the buttons to touch his chest.

"No Clint. I don't even want to go back to Mexico City anymore. But maybe I'm hoping for too much."

"Hell no! I want everything." He tilted her chin up so he could look into the eyes holding his future. "Lydia Rose Hidalgo, please stay with me. Make a life with me. Marry me." She looked stunned. So was he. He couldn't believe he actually proposed without a plan, without a ring. He was an asshole.

Her eyes filled with tears.

"I'm sorry Lydia, I didn't mean for it to come out like that."

"You don't want to marry me?"

"Of course I do. With every part of me I want you to be my wife. I just should never have blurted it out. I should have waited to propose to you with hearts and flowers, but I needed you to know now. I want you in my life forever."

"Do you really mean this?"

Clint couldn't find any more words. Just the look of her was music, was poetry. She wasn't just his future, she was his comfort, his solace, and his hope.

"I mean it, Lydia. I love you more than my life."

"I've wanted to tell you how much I love you for so long. But I didn't want you to feel pity for me. You've been so kind. I want to be your wife, but I don't know how it would work."

"We're going to make it fucking work. There is no way you're going into Witness Protection and leaving me." It was a vow.

9

"Don't make a sound."

Lydia barely heard Clint's words as he whispered in her ear. He grabbed her by the waist and helped her slip out and under the bed.

"Stay here and don't move." Again he used some freaky sub-vocal way of speaking.

The nylon carpet felt prickly against her naked body. She felt so exposed, even though there was a dust ruffle around the bed and she could barely see the floor of the bedroom.

SPLAT.

SPLAT.

What was that sound?

Oh God, it was a gun! It had a silencer.

She heard a man grunt, and then another *SPLAT.*

She heard a scream and she covered her mouth. It didn't sound like Clint. Something crashed, she heard grunts. She couldn't stand it. She scooched over to the side of the side of the bed near the door and peered under the dust ruffle. She saw boots and bare feet. She saw another body on the ground lying in a pool of blood.

One more thud, and then another clothed body hit the floor.

"Clint?"

He pulled up the ruffle and was there, looking at her. His hand grazed her face.

"Are you okay?"

"I'm fine. Stay where you are. There are probably more outside. Just give me a minute."

A minute? Was he out of his mind?

She watched as he picked up his jeans from the side of the bed and pulled them on. Then he went to the dresser and wrenched it open, pulling out his gun and his knife.

She started to count. *Uno, Dos, Tres...* She clawed at the carpet, her toes curled. After she reached sixty she started to pray. She prayed to the Virgin Mary. She would understand the beauty of Clint's soul. Mary would not allow harm to come to someone so good. She would protect him.

Lydia heard pounding feet.

"Lydia. We're leaving." Clint reached under the bed, and despite the urgency she felt from him, he was gentle as he helped her up.

"Get dressed and pack up. Whatever you do, don't use the cell phones. I think they were traced when you talked to your family. I'm getting our computers and getting anything that will be useful."

She focused on the dresser as she saw him pull the gun out of one of the dead men's hands. She was *not* going to throw up.

He came up and ran his hand down her arm. "Are you going to be all right in here while I go downstairs?"

"I'm fine. Do what you need to do so we can get the hell out of here." She went to the closet and pulled out the suitcase she unpacked that morning and started throwing clothes into it. One of the dead men was between her and the bathroom. She decided to skip the toiletries. They could buy anything they needed on the road. Sidestepping the other dead man, she went downstairs and saw Clint with his laptop open.

"Mason, we were made." Lydia went and stood behind Clint's shoulder so she could see his screen. Mason looked like he had been wakened from a dead sleep.

"Tell me."

"There were four of them. We've got to get out of here now."

"Authorities?"

"I'm not staying around for them. I need to get Lydia to safety. Tell Finn this house has been compromised."

"Don't worry about it. Get the hell out of there, and report as soon as you're someplace safe. Do you have any idea how you got made?"

"Lydia talked to both Beth and her parents today. Coordinate with Jack and Finn. My guess is we have a problem in Chicago since the Marshalls are involved. I'm ditching the cell phones and getting some burners. I'll contact you again on this secure video connection."

"How are you going to be travelling, are you taking the RV?"

"Nope. Look, we've got to go. We'll contact you in twenty-four hours. Fuck, I should never have believed those fucking Marshalls when they said the connection on their end was secure."

"You still don't know it was the phone call with her parents that caused this."

"That's bullshit, you know it didn't happen because of Jack Preston. He's too damn cautious. This is because of the fucking Marshalls. You tell Finn to throw away all of their shit and take care of the Hidalgo's security personally, otherwise Lydia isn't going to talk to them again."

Mason gave a grim nod.

"Gotta go." Clint shut the laptop. He turned to look at her.

"Fuck, I'm so fucking sorry. I fucked up." She couldn't believe her ears. She had just watched him save her life by killing two men, and apparently there were two more outside and he was apologizing for fucking up?!

"Are you out of your mind?"

"Somebody tried to kill you," he growled as he pushed up from the table and loomed over her. "It's my job to keep you safe."

"Which you did!" She shoved her finger in his chest. "My God man, let's get the hell out of here, and then we can discuss how you managed to hear shadows and save my life." He stood there for just a moment and slowly grinned.

"So you're not going to let me feel guilty?"

"Not for a second." She grinned back as she picked up the computer and shoved it at him.

"Did I tell you I want to marry you?"

"Yep, and I agreed. But if you keep trying to take the blame for shit that's not your fault, I might reconsider." She breathed a silent sigh of relief when she saw the guilt finally change to resolve.

"Wouldn't want you to change your mind." He swooped in for a hard kiss she matched. God it was like a spark to kerosene. They broke apart and he picked up the suitcase. She grabbed her laptop case and followed him out of the house. She wasn't surprised when he guided her towards a black SUV. She averted her eyes from another body.

She waited until they were on the interstate before she asked him where they were going.

"Ever wanted to go to Disney World?"

"When I was a little girl." Lydia thought back to her dreams of being a princess.

"We're going to hide near the Magic Kingdom."

"Why?"

"Orlando has a huge airport. It has Universal Studios and Epcot. We'll be invisible." It made perfect sense.

"But why does the airport matter?"

"Some of the team is going to be here eventually. We always knew you were going to be a target, but I thought it was going to be something we could arrange. This came as a total fucking surprise. The next time will be on our terms."

Despite the smile he had thrown at her as he talked about Disney World, Lydia felt him vibrating with rage. It made sense since she was beginning to tremble with the after effects.

Oh God.

"Pull over." He looked at her, and maneuvered the vehicle to the shoulder. By the time she had her seatbelt undone and the door open, he was by her side.

"I've got you." He helped her to the foliage, and had her hair pulled back as she threw up. She tried to stay upright, but it was a losing battle. When she was close to hitting her knees, he held her up, her back to his front.

Finally, there was nothing left in her stomach she

hung in his arms shuddering. It was then his tender words worked their way through to her consciousness.

"My warrior. So fierce. I have you. You're safe."

She wiped her mouth. "I'm done," she whispered weakly.

He picked her up and she was soon buckled into the passenger seat. He leaned in to kiss her, and she dodged him.

"Vomit breath."

He stole his kiss anyway.

"Always Lydia to me." She gave a watery giggle, as he probably hoped would happen. He went to his backpack and scrounged up a bottle of water and gave it to her. She sucked down a mouthful, and then motioned him out of the way so she could spit.

"Really Clint, you couldn't have waited until now to kiss me? You are such a goof."

"I'm your goof." He shut the door and they were soon back on the road. She felt better.

"Lydia, why don't you see if you can take a nap?"

"No, I want to stay up with you." That was the last thing she remembered before she fell asleep.

LYDIA DIDN'T EVEN WAKE up when he pulled over in a strip mall to buy two throw-a-way cell phones at an electronics store. He contacted Mason, and soon was getting a call from Finn.

"So how bad is it, Finn?" Clint asked quietly. He was using his newly acquired earbud so Lydia wouldn't hear anything his team mate would have to say.

"Jesus, Clint it was a blood bath up here."

"Her parents?"

"Fine. Scared to fucking death. Beth is fine too. No attempt was made on her. Her location is secure."

"Thank God. Before you tell me what happened. Have you moved locations?"

"That's a stupid question."

"So where are you?"

"On our way to Minneapolis. Damn it's going to be cold."

"Are the US Marshalls still with you?" He pulled down the visor as the sun glinted off the tractor trailer truck in front of him.

"Nope. In all of the confusion I took the Hidalgo's and left. Those dumb shits."

"Did you tell Mason?"

"Yeah, I left it up to him and our Captain to smooth things over. Mike, the guy I told you about tried to kill me tonight. I'm not going to risk the Hidalgos with them anymore. Obviously their screening system is a problem."

"Ya think?" Clint was appalled. It was like hearing a SEAL turned rogue.

"They are staying with me, and with me only, until the trial."

"Don't tell me where you are exactly."

"I wasn't planning to."

"Finn, what the hell happened?" Clint looked over at Lydia. She was still sleeping soundly.

"We have two Marshalls who patrol the house outside and two who are inside. I'm upstairs with Lydia's parents. I'm the last line of defense. It always came down to how well they've kept things under wraps. What the Marshalls didn't know is that I had put motion sensors on all of the entry points around the house, as well as one at the bottom of the stairs, since the Hidalgos and I stayed upstairs."

"Trust issues much?" Clint asked.

"Grogan seemed like a decent guy, but his organization is too big for him to know for sure he still didn't have bad apples."

"Okay, so you have the motion sensors. Then what?"

"I have the alarm set up on my phone. I knew as soon as we were breached. I got the Hidalgos into the bathroom tub. Two men were on their way upstairs by the time I got them secure. One was Mike, I didn't recognize the other. I dispatched them. When I got downstairs, I saw the other Marshall, Law Henson, were dead. I went outside. There was a van waiting. I took those motherfuckers out. They had already killed the other two Marshalls who patrolled outside."

Clint heard the fatigue in Finn's voice.

"Are you going to be able to rest?"

"Soon. Where are you headed?"

"Orlando."

"Okay, I'll text you with your accommodations."

"Bullshit. I'll figure it out. You just rest."

"Hey, you figure out the computer shit, I arrange things. We all have our strengths, me I'm the team's version of Hotels.com. After I'm done I'll get back on the road, and then when we get to Minneapolis I'll get some shut eye."

Clint relaxed. Letting Finn take care of these types of things made life better.

"Hey, Clint? Let's wait for a couple of days for Lydia to talk to her folks, okay?"

"I agree. Thanks Buddy."

CLINT PACED the floor of the suite at the Four Seasons in Orlando when a soft knock finally came. He glanced at the closed door where Lydia was sleeping before he answered the knock.

Darius and Drake nodded as he ushered them in.

"Nice digs. Who did you have to rob?" Drake went to the window and pushed back the curtain so he could look down at the view below.

"You have to ask? This is definitely Finn's doing." Darius opened the suitcase he brought in.

"Finn had to spend some time assuring me he wasn't compromised and this reservation was secure." Clint hated to question his team mate, but after the shit that went down in Tampa, he couldn't be too careful.

"Where's Lydia?" Drake asked as he peered over Darius' shoulder.

"She's sleeping." Clint pointed towards one of the closed doors in the suite.

"Are you sleeping double?" Drake asked as he took out one of the guns from the suitcase.

"Jesus, Drake, is nothing sacred?" Darius exclaimed. Then he lowered his voice and looked at Clint. "So are you?"

"You two are nothing but gossipy old ladies."

"Inquiring minds want to know."

"I asked her to marry me and she said yes."

Drake pulled out his phone and tapped on it. "Fuck!"

"What?" Clint asked.

Darius laughed. "Drake just realized he lost. Mason won the pool, right?"

"Yep. He called it."

"You guys were betting on my love life?" Clint looked at his laughing team mates as they checked out the guns and ammunition they were pulling out of the suitcase.

"Yep, it was Drake's idea," Darius said.

"You bet I was going to propose?"

"Fuck yeah. There wasn't a doubt in any of our minds, it was just a matter of when." Drake put the Beretta in the holster he was wearing.

Clint shook his head in wonder. "Where did you get the hardware?"

"Finn arranged it. A retired SEAL met us outside the airport." Darius shut the suitcase and walked over to the table where Clint had his computer set up.

"So walk us through what you have planned."

"I'm sick of being on the defensive. We need to take this to them. Lydia knows these guys. As soon as her father told them he contacted the DEA she started her own investigation. Everything was lost when she was kidnapped. Then the Marshalls kept her off the net while in the safe house, but since we've been together she's been able to put it all back together and then some."

"So how do we go on the attack?" Drake asked as he rubbed his hands together.

Clint shared a grin with Darius.

"Ricardo Hidalgo is set to testify against two DEA agents. The DA is still hoping one if not both of them will agree to turn and implicate Guzman. Once we have Guzman, we should have the link between him and the Congressman."

"And that's the reason Guzman is trying to wipe out the Hidalgos. Because he knows if the DEA agents turn, both American and Mexican officials will have what they need to take him down. We know this, so tell us something we don't know," Drake demanded.

"Lydia damn near did a colonoscopy on Guzman."

"She couldn't have gotten more than the task force they've had in the US and Mexico," Darius protested as Clint started to pull up files on his laptop.

"What she has is remarkable, and trust me, it was more." Clint's fingers flew over the keys.

"How is that possible?"

"They had people on the inside who were on the take. They were sabotaging the investigations. Lydia might have launched quite the analysis, but she didn't hack into the Mexican and US files. When I did, she was easily able to point out the missing information. It's obvious there is someone in each government who is tampering with the accumulation of evidence against Guzman's cartel."

"So what do you want to do?" Darius asked.

"I want to topple Guzman's organization. I want to make it so not everything depends on the DEA testimony." Clint turned his computer around so both men could see the pictures of Guzman and Sylvan Carter, the Congressman from Texas.

"But won't they still want the testimony so they can implicate those DEA agents?"

"Yeah, it will still necessary, but there won't be worries of reprisals if Guzman is out of the picture. So no more shit about the Witness Protection Program for Lydia's family." Clint slammed his finger against the image of the drug lord.

"What about Lydia?" Drake asked. "Were you going to join her in the program?"

"If I had to, I would. There is no way I would live my life without her. But we talked, and she wants to live a life outside of the program, even if she has to give up seeing her family. Damn guys. She's willing to give up her mom, her dad and her sister, to stay with me." Clint's voice broke.

They were all silent for a moment.

"Obviously the woman is touched in the head," Drake said, trying to lighten moment.

"Don't hate," Darius said. "One day some woman might be able to put up with your brand of bullshit."

"What are you talking about? Women love me."

"We're not talking the ones who hang out near the base and trip you to the floor. I'm talking about a woman with self-respect and a brain. Trying to get someone like that to overlook your archaic beliefs about a woman's place is going require a miracle."

"What the fuck are you talking about Dare?" Clint watched as Drake took actual offense to Darius' teasing. He tried to smooth things over.

"Look, you're my wingman when it comes to understanding a woman's mind. You know how they tick. You can cajole them out of the worst mood, and most times get them eating out of your hand. But you have to admit you tend to want women to stand behind you, not beside you."

"Fuck yeah, I do!" Drake pulled on Clint's shoulder and he shoved from his chair to stare at his friend.

"What's your problem, Drake?"

"There's nothing the fuck wrong with me wanting to protect women. I don't care whether it's my sisters, my mother God rest her soul, Mason's fiancé Sophia, your Lydia or the woman I'm going to marry. Women need to be protected. They are the most precious gift on Earth."

"Jesus Drake, I'm not disagreeing with you, Lydia is my world."

"Well then, you need to find someplace for her to hide, a hole so deep she can never get out until all of this over. She should not be trying to find Guzman! She's not fucking trained!"

"Drake, it's so good to see you again." They all looked up to see Lydia standing in the open doorway. She was wrapped in the bed's down comforter, her black hair tumbling all around her. She looked young, delicate, and in need of protection. Maybe Drake was right.

"Baby, I'm sorry we woke you."

"You didn't, Drake did." She walked over to where Drake was standing, the comforter dragged on the floor behind her.

"I can't decide if you need to be kicked in the nuts or need a hug."

Drake just stood there with a cold and forbidding look on his face.

"I've been listening to the shit you've been spouting. I don't know what happened to a woman you loved in the past, but you can't wrap all of us in cotton wool."

"You don't know what the fuck you're talking about," Drake snarled at Lydia.

"Drake, I will happily pay the hotel cleaning charges to beat the hell out of you if you don't start speaking to Lydia with the utmost respect." It took everything Clint had not to take a swing at his friend, but he knew Lydia would kill him.

"All I'm saying is I know you mean well." Lydia continued staring at Drake. "If I didn't know your intentions were good and honorable, I couldn't stand being around you. But you *do* mean well, so that means we are going to have to figure out how to work together." She gripped the comforter even tighter. "I might not have military training, but I'm capable of assisting in this investigation. My father is the reason you all are involved, and I demand to be part of the solution."

"Lydia, you almost died yesterday," Drake's voice was pained, almost pleading. "Clint loves you too much to deny you anything. But I have more perspective. You stay here, and we'll go to the front lines so to speak."

"No." Her voice quiet and firm.

"What the fuck do you mean 'no'?" Drake looked at her like she was speaking a foreign language.

"I mean where Clint goes, I go."

"You'll be a liability."

She turned all of her attention to Clint. "Will I? Because if I will, then I'll do what Drake suggests. I would never let my pride put you in harm's way."

He pulled her into his arms, carefully making sure the comforter stayed in place. He was pretty sure she was naked underneath, and he sure as hell didn't want to share all of that beauty with Darius and Drake. He used the moment to formulate his answer.

"Lydia, as long as you listen to what I say, and stay put when I need you to, then this will work out fine. You already know I think all the information you provided is invaluable. What's more, as things start to escalate I think you staying on top of your network of sources will be critical."

She pressed closer to him.

"You are so fucking pussy whipped, Clint." Drake groaned.

"You are so fucking jealous, Drake." Darius laughed.

LYDIA WATCHED out of the corner of her eye as Clint let himself into the room they shared.

"Why are you getting dressed?"

Lydia stood up straight and tried to unobtrusively adjust herself into the cups of her bra. Apparently it wasn't working, because Clint was staring.

"I'm getting dressed because we have guests."

"Huh?" How in the hell could a big man move as fast as he could? He was suddenly in front of her staring down at the light blue silk of her underwire bra. Men were obsessed with breasts, that's all there was to it.

"I'll be out in a minute, why don't you go back out there with Drake and Darius."

"They've left." He slipped the straps of her bra down her arms.

"I thought they were staying in the suite with us."

"According to Drake, Finn knew we would want privacy." She leaned her forehead against his chest. She didn't know whether to be embarrassed or thankful. She'd figure it out later. She tried to lift her arms to start unbuttoning his shirt, but her arms were bound to her sides by her lingerie. Lydia began to unlatch her bra, when Clint stayed her hands.

"Leave it." He bent and picked her up and placed her on the huge bed. He had a wild look in his eyes. She'd seen it on and off since the shooting. There was no hint of her playful lover.

After the conversation with Drake it all made sense. Clint was holding on by a thread. He had the exact same instincts as Drake, he wanted to hide her away someplace safe. He just hid his caveman side better than Drake did. Last night probably terrified him.

She tried to lift her arms to offer him solace, but once again realized she was trapped by the straps of her bra.

"Please let me take this off."

"On one condition," Clint said. She never heard his voice so deep before. It was as if it was coming from a place deep in his core.

"What?"

"You do whatever I say tonight. I almost lost you and it's eating me alive. Will you do this?" Damn, she could see he was unsure, and it about killed her.

"Clint, we're still new to one another. But know this. Whenever it is within my power to give to you, I will always provide what you need." He framed her face, his eyes assessing, finally he nodded. Peeling off her bra, he took her hands so they touched the suede headboard.

"Keep your hands there, okay baby?" Lydia swallowed and nodded.

Clint got off the bed and stripped, then slid her panties down and off her legs. He stood beside the bed and looked down at her for long, long moments.

Lydia's nipples tightened and her mouth watered as Clint's erect flesh came into view. She was pretty sure tonight wasn't just about making love for Clint, it was about him needing to claim her. For her, it was an affirmation of life.

She never saw men battle before. Hearing the gunshots, seeing the dead body in their bedroom, and then having Clint go outside had frightened her to death. Intellectually she knew he was a capable soldier, a SEAL, but she was scared out of her mind he was going to die.

This was their first time to really be close again, and she needed everything he could give her.

"Lydia, will you keep your hands where I told you?"

"Yes," she breathed out softly.

He sat down beside her and splayed his hand out on her stomach. She looked down and loved seeing how they looked together. Masculine to feminine. His hand made her feel so safe, but then he stroked through her curls, and parted her intimate flesh, his fingers met with a warm wet welcome.

"Baby, you couldn't be any more perfect." He delved further and sank inside her. "Spread your legs for me."

Lydia shuddered at the carnal request. She wanted to do what he asked. She wanted to give him exactly what seemed to so desperately need, but years of conditioning made it so difficult.

"Lydia, I love your body, and the idea of you showing it to me, pleases me."

As if he uttered a magic phrase, Lydia parted her legs. Dots hovered around the edges of her vision as she forgot to breathe.

"You mean everything to me. Pleasuring you...loving you...keeping you safe...will be my life's work."

Clint loved her gently at first, his hand, fingers and tongue a symphony on her flesh guiding her ever upwards. As she soared, he demanded more from her, his strokes turning even more powerful, her body's responses were not her own. She didn't even know pleasure could be so brutal or she could embrace such need, such a frenzy of passion.

"Again," he demanded.

"I can't," she said as her hands finally moved to touch his head.

His green eyes glittered upwards. "Do you want me to stop? Really?"

"No! I need you inside me. Please, I need us together this time." Then she saw the real Clint. Ah God, he was feeling guilty. Just for an instant, she saw the emotion flash across his face. That was why he was denying himself. Not on her watch!

"Please, you promised to give me what I needed. You promised, Clint." He hesitated.

"Lydia, I–"

"We love each other. The only way this will ever work is if we are both here for each other. Please love, please, I'm begging you. Let me be here for you too." She watched as he struggled. He bent his head to her tummy.

"I can't lose you, Lydia."

"You denying us, will tear us apart." She ran her fingers through his hair, and then tugged so he was forced to look at her. "You know this. You know you saved me. I know I'm always going to be able to depend on you."

"But it was so close." His breathing was ragged.

She pulled out the big guns.

"Not only do I trust you with my life, I trust you with our children's lives. We are all going to be safe with you watching over us Clint Anthony Archer."

He went wild. He pulled her hands away from his head and pressed them back against the headboard.

"Now keep them there."

His lips bit kisses all over her body. She writhed against him, she couldn't get close enough. Vaguely she noted him finally putting on protection, happy they were finally going to make love, but sad there needed to be a barrier between them. Still the man hesitated.

"Clint, don't make me beg."

"Never." He slid against her entrance and she jerked upwards. He held her down. "We agreed my way tonight." He waited for her nod.

Lydia reveled in his gentle advancements, she had no recourse but to try to tempt him with her body, and hold him tight so he would stay.

"You're killing me." Clint's expression was grim, as he tried to continue to go slow, but Lydia was as determined he go fast. She was desperate for the feel of her man. She closed her eyes, concentrating on their joined bodies, and moisture pulsed in welcome.

"Fuck!" Clint lunged and Lydia cried with rapture. But even then Clint gave her a quick look of concern, and flipped them over so she was on top. Soon they were twisting and twining their bodies merged, both trying to please the other. Finally thought was no longer possible, only feeling was left, and they skyrocketed to another dimension, safe in one another's arms.

LYDIA WAS STILL TRYING to figure out if it felt totally wrong, or totally right to be sitting up naked in bed next to Clint with her laptop and headset talking to one of her shadiest friends.

She would have preferred to be making love yet again, but Clint refused. He insisted she needed to rest. The damn man was right, she was physically exhausted, but she felt fantastic. She'd tried to sleep, but her eyes refused to close. She finally wheedled enough so she could see what she had missed on-line for the last two days. That's when she'd seen the messages from Melvin.

Clint had his computer in his lap, supposedly he was

going to work as well, but once again he seemed to be ogling her breasts. She'd asked him if he was going to always do that. He said in sixty years it was possible he might stop, but he doubted it. She did her best to block out Clint so she could focus on what Melvin was saying.

"No, I told you, I can't video skype tonight, Melvin. You'll just have to cope with audio."

"But seeing your beautiful face is one of the things that gets me through the day, my gorgeous kitten." Lydia rolled her eyes at Clint.

"If your information is good, we'll video skype next week." Clint gave her a steely look and shook his head. Yeah, she didn't think it would work anymore. Melvin was pretty sleazy, but he always had the best information. So what if she smiled and wore tight sweaters to help get that info?

"Okay my kitten, here is what you needed to know. Guzman's son Berto is trying to win Daddy's love, and the apple didn't fall far from the tree."

"Sure, I know about Berto, but he's never really been on my radar. Why are you mentioning him?"

"Because Daddy told him if he got rid of your dad and the rest of you he would get to take over some new venture. They are calling it Operation Omega. I guess daddy has an end game in mind." Lydia felt gooseflesh begin to form, but then Clint put his arm around her and it helped make her feel better.

"Why isn't Guzman taking care of it himself? Why is he relegating this to Berto?"

"Word on the street is he wants to continue to run the drug side of the business, but he wants his son to spearhead this new venture."

"So is Berto behind the hits?"

"He has friends that are basically psychos. But Berto was behind it all right."

"What proof do you have?"

"Berto's friends are novices on the dark web. They have been doing a lot of recruiting out there, and also buying and selling illegal weapons. They've been stupid enough to have mentioned their friend BG. They went further to explain about a hit they were doing in Florida and in Illinois for BG. What do you think? Sounds like evidence to me." Melvin sounded like he was doing the pee-pee dance he was so excited.

"Do you have this backed up?"

"It's being sent to your secure drop account as we speak, Kitten. I've been waiting for you to connect with me before I sent it over to you. I wanted to make sure you were safe and it would be you who would pick it up."

The man was pragmatic. He wouldn't want anyone to be able to trace back the information to him if her accounts were being monitored by the Guzman's.

"Is there anything else I need to be aware of?"

"You need to talk to Sylvia. I track guns and drugs. She's the one who tracks dirty money. You might have to have your new friend video skype with her to get the information you're going to need." Lydia frowned, Sylvia was like Melvin from a female perspective she *really* liked her men. At least that's the part she played.

Sylvia Hessman was a player at the same level as Melvin, only she had a high profile RL, real life, presence. Lydia knew Sylvia Hessman was just a character the woman played. Kind of like an avatar. She'd tried to run a deep background check on her, but hadn't been able to find out who Sylvia really was. Bottom line, she was someone who knew where all the financial bodies were buried, and she occasionally came out and played.

Sylvia would eat Clint up with a spoon. Then she realized what Melvin just said.

"Hey! How do you know about my new friend?"

"There's a picture on the web of you two leaving the hospital in Dallas. I figure he's probably still there with you and that's why I don't get to do the video skype thing." Lydia was already logged into her secure drop account.

"Send me the picture. Has he been identified?"

"Negative. He was wearing a ball cap that covered his features. He acted like a pro. Built like one too. Sylvia's going to be chomping at the bit to bring him over to the dark side."

"He's mine. She can't have him." Melvin let out a loud laugh. Clint grinned and hugged her closer.

"Lydia, I'm just telling you what will be the best bait to use for the information you want to get." Her computer pinged and she pulled up a bunch of JPEG images. She was clearly visible. She looked like a stiff wind would blow her away, which just made Clint look all the more powerful. But Melvin was right, the ball cap covered his face. She covered her mic.

"Did you know we were under surveillance?"

"It's best to assume we are. That's why when we changed vehicles you had the scarf over your head and sunglasses on." She uncovered the microphone.

"Melvin, where is Sylvia hanging out these days?"

"You can reach her at her normal hangouts on the dark net. If push comes to shove, you can always message her dummy account on Facebook."

"No, I mean where is she in real life?" Lydia's question was met by the sound of keys tapping.

"Are you sure about this, Lydia? Sylvia is as scary in her way as that fucker Berto. She has real blood on her hands."

"I'm sure."

"That guy who's with you. Is he on the up and up? Will he be able to protect you? I'm assuming he's right there with you."

"Yeah, he's with me. So are some of his friends. They're the good guys, and they can be pretty damn scary too. I can't tell you anything more. I don't want you messed up in this, Melvin."

"I intend to be, and not just because I got to see your cleavage every other week. I know all about you Lydia Hidalgo. I have always thought you were crazy to want to join the Federal Ministerial Police. In my opinion, you're too good for them. But I always admired the fact you wanted to do good. So there is no way I am not going to help you when you most need it."

"All I need from you is Sylvia's whereabouts."

"I'll give you everything I have on her. But I'll continue to ferret out other information as it comes to light and feed it to your secure drop account."

"Melvin, how good is your security?" Lydia kicked herself for never having asked this before.

"Kitten, ain't no one ever going to find your Uncle Melvin."

"Ooooohh. That's just nasty. Please never refer to yourself as my uncle again, okay?"

"See, now you're not worried about me anymore. Check your account tomorrow, you'll have everything you need about our dear cousin Sylvia then."

"Enough with the family references, you're creeping me out."

"Ciao, Kitten." The line went dead.

They put their computers on the nightstands beside the bed. "I still don't know what we're going to do about Sylvia."

"Let's not borrow trouble. We'll see what your friend Melvin sends us. It could be that he can't find anything on her, so it's a moot point."

"I haven't told you much about Melvin, but he's seriously good. He'll find out about Sylvia. When he does, we'll need to be ready. But just so you know, as much as you disliked the idea of me flirting with Melvin, same goes. I don't want you letting Sylvia sinking her claws into you." Instead of arguing, Clint just gave her a very satisfied smile.

"You're jealous."

"Nope, I just don't share well with others." Clint fluffed up the pillows and positioned them so that they were cuddled facing one another.

"I applaud the sentiment. Please remember I feel the same way. If you have any other contacts you video skype with, plan to stop. Also, quit with the sexy voice when you're talking to poor Melvin." She opened her mouth to protest, but Clint raised his eyebrow.

"Okay, no more sexy voice."

"I didn't say stop it entirely, just with your contacts." She laughed. "Now scooch closer, I need to feel you against me. I can't get to sleep without you in my arms." She nestled closer, loving the smell of him, and the feel of his hand on her ribcage.

"Maybe..."

"No more maybes tonight. You plumb wore me out Lydia."

She giggled. Not even the thought of Sylvia and the

Guzman's could ruin perfection of sleeping in Clint's arms.

———

CLINT HATED the fact Sylvia insisted on meeting Lydia face-to-face. Clint insisted on meeting her far-the-fuck-away from Orlando, so they were now in Houston. In fact, were at the bar in the St. Regis Hotel in Downtown Houston, and he couldn't imagine anything bad going down here.

However, there was an upside, he got to see Drake hating life as he was dressed in a charcoal gray Armani suit with a silk maroon shirt. He never saw Drake this uncomfortable, and it was providing him and Darius unending joy. It had been Lydia's idea to make Sylvia lose focus. What the hell, a beautiful woman often worked to make him lose focus, at least they had before Lydia came into his life. Darius was waiting upstairs in yet another magnificent suite Finn arranged. They had a microphone set up so he could hear everything said at the table.

A tiny blonde woman glided into the wood paneled bar on the tallest high heels imaginable. She was wearing a black pinstripe suit that hugged every curve. Her hair was slicked back in some kind of complicated elegant braid.

"Lydia Hidalgo, it's so nice to meet you." Sylvia Grant sat down in one of the wingback chairs and crossed her legs. Clint could see the tops of her stockings, he glanced over at Drake. He easily read his friend. Drake was both salivating and offended. Damn, friend was a piece of work.

Sylvia raised her hand and a waiter literally ran over

to take her order. She stroked her hand down the waiter's arm and then turned to Drake.

"And can I have him bring you anything, handsome?"

"I'm capable of ordering my own beverages, thank you." Drake gave her a cold look. Well now he was outraged.

"But I thought you were brought here for my benefit, or did I misread things? I don't work for free."

Before Clint or Drake could even form an answer, Lydia was in Sylvia's face.

"Sylvia, I expected better of you, but I'm saving my evaluation until after our meeting is completed. In the meantime, listen very carefully. Just because you're a woman and he's a man, doesn't mean the same rules don't apply. I'm allowed to bring eye-candy to butter you up and make the meeting go smoother, but everyone at this table is free and belong to themselves. They will not be coerced or paid to do anything abhorrent to them. Now pull down your damn skirt, you'll scare the customers."

"Lydia–" Drake started.

Lydia held up her hand, her eyes never leaving Sylvia's face. Finally, Sylvia nodded.

"She's right. I apologize." Sylvia uncrossed her legs, tucked them tightly together and tugged at her skirt.

What the fuck just happened? He looked over at his woman, but she was still staring at Sylvia. Sylvia looked back at her.

"So you're a friend of Melvin's too? How'd you meet him?" Sylvia asked.

"I was doing a research paper for my Criminology class. I needed some information on how information was being hijacked out of company Ethernet despite their firewalls and security."

"Yes, Melvin's your guy for that."

"We talked for months, and then he turned me onto the dark net, and all things related with human trafficking, drug trade, and illegal arms. I was interested in the Mexican cartels, specifically Alfonso Guzman, so I focused on drugs."

"You're being naïve; he's got his hands in all of those other pies as well."

"Not human trafficking," Lydia protested.

"Is it illegal? Does it make money? Than Guzman is doing it."

"What's your angle? I finally figured out Melvin's."

"Oh really, what did you figure out about Melvin?"

The waiter came back, and this time everyone ordered for themselves.

"It's private. If he hasn't told you, I don't want to break a confidence," Lydia said.

"Fair enough." Sylvia played with the napkin the waiter put down on the table.

"You're on the side of angels Lydia, I've checked out you and your merry men. So I feel comfortable telling you I'm going to retire within the next twelve months. Sylvia Hessman will no longer exist."

"Why does she exist in the first place?"

Clint really looked at the woman, and realized she wore a lot of make-up. *A lot* of make-up. She had made herself look much older than she was. Lydia was twenty-four, but he was thinking this woman was probably four or five years younger.

"My angle is simple. I make money by following the stock market. All of these criminal assholes have their money tied up in banks and corporations. I watch their illegal business, I see how their operations are doing, I know how it will impact their legal businesses, and voila, I will make good trades."

Her hand trembled as she reached for her drink. It was subtle, but he looked over at Drake and realized that he had seen it as well.

"If you're only in it for the money, why are you here talking to Lydia?" Clint asked.

"Sylvia is only in it for the money. Like Melvin I have my own story. Helping Lydia is something that makes the real me happy." She took a sip of her whiskey and Clint saw her put on a blank face. Obviously Sylvia liked whiskey but the real girl didn't. Fuck, this was all too confusing for him.

"What should we call you?"

"Sylvia!" Both women said in unison.

"Clint, anything else gets her killed."

Drake lifted his hand and asked for the bill. He got out his wallet and pulled out a wad of cash. When the waiter gave him the ticket, Drake eyes widened. He handed it to Clint.

"We're going to be charging it to his suite."

How could four drinks cost that much? Then he saw the price of Sylvia's whiskey. For God's sakes, she didn't even like the stuff. He signed the tab.

"We're moving this party upstairs Sylvia."

———

DARIUS WAS in the room waiting for them. He took one look at Sylvia and he started frowning.

"For God's sake, you're a baby."

"I'm five feet, one inches tall," Sylvia said indignantly.

"Are you even twenty?"

"I'm thirty." Clint and Drake both laughed. The girl had guts. Lydia started really looking at Sylvia. Now that they weren't in the low light of the bar, she saw all the make-up she was wearing. If her hair wasn't pulled back in such a severe hair-style, then her baby face would really be noticeable.

"You're the contact that brought us to Houston. The one who is the barracuda who was going to eat Drake alive?" Darius sounded exasperated. He put his arm around her and guided her towards the couch.

"Get your hands off me, Mr. Stanton." She tried to shrug out of his hold, but it did no use, as he had her sitting at the couch before she could finish her protest.

"That's Master Chief Stanton. How in the hell do you women walk in these shoes? How do you know my name?" He pulled them off her feet and she let out a sigh of pleasure.

"Damn, Dare, quit manhandling our guest."

"I know all of you. My business is information. I suppose you were listening to our conversation?"

"Yep, I heard it all. You're one of the good guys. Or good girls. So we have to take care of you." He started to massage her foot. Sylvia gaped at him.

"Y'all are bat shit crazy. I just wanted to meet Lydia, make sure she was on the up-and-up. If she was, then I was going to tell her what I knew, and start supplying her with info going forward. I'm not signing up with y'all. I work alone." The last was said with a distinct Southern accent.

"So did we pass the test?" Lydia asked.

"Yes, you did. These men you're surrounded by haven't. How in the hell do you stand them? They're like steam rollers." She shot a glare over

"Look, let me give you my information and then get back home. I should have known it was a bad idea to meet with the likes of y'all. I should have just trusted my instincts and done this all online."

The accent was getting thicker by the minute and she looked so forlorn. Clint crouched in front of her.

"Why *did* you meet with us honey?"

"What I found out for Mizz Lydia scared me. Melvin normally finds out all of the criminal stuff, I find the money stuff. But I found a video hidden away. It was awful." She twisted her fingers in her lap, and Lydia covered them with her own. She looked up at Lydia with tears in her blue eyes.

"I only saw part of the video before it was taken down. I thought they would trace back to me, but I put up enough walls that they couldn't find me. I'm so sorry I didn't copy it."

"What happened?"

"They tor-tor-tortured this man. They cut him...open. They were pulling..." She stopped and gagged. Darius was there with a glass of water. Sylvia took it gratefully and sipped.

"He died. The man who did it had a mask. He told the camera that if they didn't tell them the location of Ricardo Hidalgo that this is what would happen to his family."

"Lydia, I know you, we are part of the same online community. I had to find you and tell you. I had to warn you." She gagged again. She lurched up off the couch and looked around wildly.

"The bathroom is this way." Lydia put her arm around her, and guided her down the hall at a run.

"Fuck. Who are these people?" Dare asked.

"What are you talking about? What else would you expect from Guzman?" Drake snarled.

"No, you dumb fuck. Lydia, this Melvin guy, and now this brave girl. Who are these people who are basically fighting evil? I mean we're soldiers, we are trained for this shit, but they all got involved and they're right in the middle of it."

"I still can't believe I didn't notice how young she was," Drake said as he rubbed the back of his neck. "She had me running scared. I was ready to go join a convent, and then I find out she's just a baby."

"It's pretty fucking funny if you ask me." Clint watched as Drake ripped off the silver tie and pulled off his suit coat. They heard the women coming back from the bathroom. Sylvia looked totally different, all of her make-up had been wiped off, and she now looked like a fresh faced farm girl.

"Where are you from?" Drake asked, playing up his own Tennessee accent.

"Texas born and bred."

"Do your parents know you're out this late?"

"Ah fuck, here we go," Darius muttered.

"I beg your pardon?"

"Shouldn't you be studying for your finals, so you get to go to homecoming? Does Dad know you're running around downtown Houston? Who do I need to call? I know you think you're the big bad, but you are not going to risk your life on my watch." Drake pulled his phone out of his pocket and took her picture before she had a chance to move. He pressed another couple of buttons.

"Clint, I just sent you her pic, do me a favor and track down Nancy Drew. I want her back home and in bed by midnight."

"Thanks ever so sir," she said sarcastically. "Mom and Dad are dead. But the last foster father I had would love to have me back in my bed so he could come and visit. Is that what you want for me? Is it?"

"That's not where you're staying now, is it?" That was Drake, never backing down.

"Fuck no! That was four years ago."

"So you have someplace safe you could be? Somewhere not in the middle of trying to take down international drug smugglers?"

"Yes! And as soon as I'm done giving Lydia, *not you*, my information you will never find me again."

"Bullshit. You now belong to us. You will be under our care."

"Are you out of your ever-loving-mind?" She turned to Lydia who shrugged. She turned to Clint who grimaced. Then she turned to Darius who looked poleaxed. She turned back to Drake.

"You are a special kind of stupid, aren't you Drake Avery. Not only do I take care of myself. I'm the one who takes care of others."

"Look missy." A shrill whistle sounded. Everyone turned to Darius.

"Enough," Darius said quietly.

"He started it."

"Well I'm finishing it. Drake get Sylvia's computer from her room. She needs to get Lydia some information."

"How do you know I have a room here?" Darius raised an eyebrow. Her shoulders drooped. She handed her room key to Drake.

"Don't let her leave while I'm gone."

"Shut up Drake, you've done enough damage."

As Drake shut the door behind him, the four of them stood in a circle in the middle of the room.

"I hate being the shortest. I hate having everyone looking down on me."

"We're not looking down on you, I promise. You just gave Drake hell, as far as I'm concerned I'm looking up to you." Clint grinned.

Darius bent down to the coffee table and picked up the room service menu. "Sylvia, do you trust us enough to tell us your real name?"

"Rylie Jones."

"So you only trust us halfway?"

"Huh? Oh no." She laughed. "Jones is my real last name. I suppose we have to tell the caveman right?"

"He's a good guy, just overzealous," Lydia explained.

"Okay Rylie Jones, what would you like me to order from room service?" Darius asked as he held up the menu.

"Anything that gets out the taste of vomit and whiskey. What are their desserts? Do they have strawberry shortcake?"

"I've got Sylvia's computer, and I want prime rib if you're placing an order from room service."

"She's not Sylvia anymore." Lydia pulled the computer out of Drake's hands and put it on the dining room table in the suite.

"Huh, what'd I miss?" Darius was on the phone and Rylie was standing next to Lydia. Clint explained the name change.

"So just go easy on the girl."

"I'll be more than happy to go easy on her, as long as I'm assured she is leaving here to go someplace safe."

They all worked late into the night going over all of Rylie's information. It was clear Guzman wanted Ricardo

Hidalgo dead. By midnight it became clear why he was so intent on his goal.

"Oh my God. The DEA agent that Papa is going to testify against was involved in not just drugs but in human trafficking."

"Yep. That means if he rolls over, he'll implicate Guzman not just on drugs but on sexual slavery."

"No wonder they want Papa dead."

After that revelation, they decided it was time to call it quits.

"I'm exhausted. I need to go to my room."

"Are you okay?" Lydia asked.

"Yeah, this was great," she said slowly. "It's weird working with others. I'm so used to working on my own." Rylie gave a rueful smile to the others around the table. Lydia was happy to see Rylie was at least considering working with her and the SEAL team in the future.

"Rylie, we'll talk about how you could work with us more going forward in the morning. I'll walk you to your room tonight." Lydia saw Rylie bristle, but then she calmed down.

"Okay, Drake. What time should I be here?"

"We'll order room service for breakfast. Why not eight o'clock?"

Rylie went over to the couch to pick up her shoes. Darius was there before her.

"Don't wear them, just carry them. The hallways all have carpet." Rylie looked into Darius' brown eyes and nodded.

"Come on girl, let's get a move on." Drake had her laptop under his arm and the door open waiting for her.

In retrospect Lydia realized they should have known

she acquiesced too easily. She wasn't in the hotel the next morning.

"You're the computer guru's," Darius growled at Clint and Lydia. "Find her."

Lydia turned her computer screen around so Darius could see what she found on-line. It was Rylie Jones' obituary. It was from four years ago. She apparently died when the small home she lived in with her foster parents burned down. The parents and three other children who were living there survived.

The picture of Rylie looked very close to the woman they met yesterday. She had hardly aged. She'd just turned seventeen when she'd supposedly died.

"Look up Roger Edwards, the foster father. What happened to him?" Clint was already searching through his computer before Darius finished asking the question.

"He's currently serving time in prison for statutory rape."

"What happened to wife and the other children?"

"The wife remarried. The foster kids are living with a single older woman. It's not the best set-up, but at least they're together."

"We have to find her."

"We will," Clint assured him. "She's going to make a mistake as she's feeding us information, so we'll get her. In the meantime, we have to get Lydia back to Orlando. I never felt good about having her here in Houston."

10

LYDIA DIDN'T KNOW HOW SHE COULD BE FEELING NERVOUS, happy and frustrated all at the same time, but she was. She looked over at Clint, and he seemed calm. Great, now she was pissed off too.

"Calm down baby, it's going to be fine."

"We should be there with them."

"We're exactly where we should be." He waved towards the castle.

"Disney World? Are you out of your mind? I should have never let you talk me into going there." They had spent the morning at the park, now they were lounging on the hotel balcony.

"It was fun. We needed to take a break."

"But we weren't doing anything." And it was driving her insane. It was five days since they met with Rylie, and Clint hustled her back to Orlando. Okay, granted spending time with Clint was a dream come true. She loved getting to know him even better.

"Clint, you're not listening to me. We need to help

your team mates. Also, we haven't heard from Rylie and it's killing me."

"Lydia, the plan was always to keep you safe. We're hiding. We're keeping you safe."

"But we're not helping. You said we were going to take down Guzman."

Clint finally put down his e-reader and turned to give her his full attention.

"Weren't we up until the wee hours of the morning doing a lot of digging on the net and dark web gathering intel?"

Lydia blushed. They *had* been up until the wee hours of the morning, but only partly because of the investigation.

"Baby, I love it when you turn that delightful shade of rose. It tells me you're thinking of the wonderful naughty things we've done together." He reached out and ran his hand down the length of her leg, since she was wearing a bikini.

"Don't try to change the subject. We've been here for five days. We haven't heard from your team in over twenty-four hours. What's going on?"

"You know they're running an operation down in Mexico City. The intelligence we got from Melvin about the shipment coming in tonight was phenomenal. The problem is, our guys don't know who they can trust. Our captain was able to pull in another SEAL team, so Mason, Drake and Darius aren't alone. They're going to be fine."

"But you said this bust won't stop Guzman unless he's there, or unless one of his people rolls over on him."

"That's true. But this will definitely put him on the ropes. This shipment is probably four month's worth of production. He will make mistakes trying to recoup his losses."

"But shouldn't we have been in Mexico City to talk to the people they do take into custody? After all, I know his operation, I could–"

"Lydia, that's out of the question. There's a hit out on you. If they see you, they will kill you." Clint's eyes glittered gray and she knew he was serious.

"All right, all right." She heard the computer ping in the other room. She got up from the couch.

"I can feel you watching me you know."

"Watching you is my favorite pastime." Lydia could actually feel his gaze on her, and he was definitely *not* looking at the scars on her back, he was looking at her ass. It was like his eyes were actually touching her there. She shook her head at her wayward thoughts.

She pulled on a sweatshirt and sat down to look at her computer. Apparently Rylie must have heard her talking about her, because she just got some information from the Sylvia Hessman account.

"Clint," Lydia called out, "Rylie just downloaded some information. Do you want to try to trace it back or do you want me to?"

She admired how fast and graceful he moved as he picked up his laptop and sat down next to her.

"See if you can get her to engage in a conversation. I'll track her."

The little apartment was quiet except for the sound of fingers tapping on the keyboards.

"She's sorry she worried us."

"Keep her talking baby." Lydia looked down at the words on the screen, imagining the young woman out there on her own. She'd been so scared when she saw the information she delivered. She actually had a name of yet another DEA agent who was compromised. It looked like this DEA agent had a junkie sister who was currently being held hostage by the Guzman organization. How the hell did Rylie manage to find this shit out?

"Do you have her?"

"I've got her IP address pinpointed to Oklahoma."

"Hurry, she's getting suspicious." Lydia asked Rylie another question, but she ended the conversation.

"Fuck!" Clint slammed the palm of his hand against the back of the couch.

"What?"

"Not only did she stop sending e-mails, she shut down the account. Dammit!"

"What's the problem, you said you had her IP address pinpointed."

"Just to her provider, not down to her address."

Lydia stared at Clint. "You're scary, you could have done that?"

"Yes, if she hadn't actually shut down her account. *Rylie* is scary."

"Okay, we are soooo damn lucky. Somehow she is using one of the smallest service providers in the country. Not one of the biggies. This must mean she lives in the sticks."

"Oh God," Lydia moaned. "Call Mason, call him now." Clint was off the couch and dialing his lieutenant before Lydia said anything else. He rushed back as she turned her laptop around. He scanned her screen as his phone rang.

"Mase, call me." He pressed end, then dialed another number as he continued to read. Lydia got up and wrapped her arm around his waist.

Somebody must have answered, because Clint started talking.

"Drake, you've been made. It's a trap."

Clint looked at Lydia and then tapped his phone and it was on speaker.

"Are you sure? From our side, it looks good."

"We got data from Rylie. It's another video. Guzman uses those to warn his people against betraying him. The video was real and brutal. This guy admitted to having sold out the time and place of the drop."

"Thanks for the intel. Gotta go." The line went dead.

"Will he let us know what happened?"

"We'll be his first call, I promise you." He hugged her. Lydia couldn't get close enough to him. Then she burst into tears.

"Oh baby, it's going to be all right. They're SEALs. Rylie's a hero. She saved them."

———

THEY ORDERED A PIZZA. It tasted like the cardboard box that it came in. How long did it take for his team mates to back out of a situation? All they had to do was cancel the op, and then call him. Instead it had been four hours. What the fuck?

Lydia tried to offer him some comfort. She cuddled close to him on the couch, but it was as if his nerve endings were on the outside of his skin and her touching him felt like nails on a chalkboard. Thank God she understood. He couldn't believe how much he loved her.

That had been an hour ago. Now she was dinking with one of the speakers from the stereo system. She had it apart and seemed to be doing something with the amplifier. He remembered when she asked to pick up some tools from the electronics store and he had said it would be cheaper to buy a new speaker.

"But fixing the speaker provides me entertainment."

He couldn't argue with her. He had an added bonus of being able to borrow her tools.

His phone rang. He put it on speaker.

"We got them!" It was Mason.

Clint leaned against the wall, a silly grin on his face.

"Damn, Mase, I should've realized you were going to use the intel to your advantage."

"What the hell? Have you been worrying about us the entire time? Come on, this hiding bullshit has messed with your brain. Of course we used it. It went even better than our original plan!" Clint heard the glee in his commander's voice.

"There was minimal bloodshed and no deaths."

"Who got hurt?" Lydia asked.

"Nobody from our side," Mason assured her.

"So you should be able to turn someone."

"I don't know," Mason's voice turned somber. I got the video that the girl Rylie sent. That is some sick shit."

"Yeah. I hated Lydia had to see it." Lydia glared at him. "Well I do, so sue me."

"Anyway, the men are more afraid of Guzman than anything the authorities can dish out. I really don't know if they will roll on him." With those words Lydia stopped glaring, instead she slumped in defeat. Clint held out his arms and Lydia walked into them. He held her close, her head tucked against his neck.

"How many did you capture?"

"We got five of his top guys. Fourteen in all."

Lydia twisted so she could speak in the phone.

"Mason, I'm so glad you're okay. When do you get to go home?"

"Soon, probably tomorrow. Sophia's birthday is Saturday, so I'll be able to make it. I was worried I would miss it." Clint could hear the relief in his friend's voice.

"That's good."

"Hey, we've got some prisoners to process. Captain Hale is flying in tonight to help smooth things with the Mexican authorities. Despite the good news that such a big drug bust was made, they are *not* happy the US Navy was responsible."

"I think Clint, Melvin and I can help."

"How?"

"I'm not quite sure. But we should be able to leave a trail that you were contacted, and make it look like it was from internal Mexican sources."

There was a long pause.

"That could work."

"Mase, you go do what you have to do, and let Lydia and I get to work."

"Roger that."

His stomach growled. Lydia laughed, she kissed the side of his mouth.

"I'll go heat up the pizza you didn't eat." He grabbed her before she had a chance to start towards the kitchen.

"Thanks for putting up with me."

"Huh?" She looked genuinely perplexed.

"I was being an asshole earlier. You were trying to offer me comfort and I blew you off."

"Geez Clint, you needed some space. I get that." She squeezed him, and it felt wonderful. "I love you. You get to be snarly sometimes. I get to be bitchy sometimes. As long as we don't make a habit of it, we're good."

"Let's hold off on the pizza." He bent down and brushed her lips with his. He loved her lush response. His hands traced downwards and cupped her butt. She felt wonderful. His stomach growled again, and she started laughing. The mood was broken.

"I'm sorry. I'm sorry. Let's get you fed first, okay big guy?" She was still giggling as she sauntered into the kitchen. As he watched her ass sway, he planned to make this the shortest meal in history.

———

CLINT WAS FEELING proud of himself the next day. Not for having provided the cover for Mason and the team, it was something he and Lydia accomplished together. No, what he was proud of, was having convinced Lydia to go to bed early.

According to the doctors, patients recovering from pneumonia should still be taking it easy for a couple of months after they left the hospital. She sure as hell didn't do that. She was eating better and gained some weight, but all of the bullshit she had endured since leaving the hospital hadn't been conducive to resting. So Clint was gloating that she actually went to bed before nine p.m.

His phone vibrated in his pocket, and he saw it was San Antonio. Beth was just going to have to wait to talk to her sister.

"Hi Beth," Clint answered the phone.

"Clint, it's me Jack."

"What's wrong?" There was something in Jack's voice that had every one of his instincts on high alert.

"Beth was bit by a snake. It's bad. She's in the ICU."

"Is she going to live?"

Jack cleared his throat. "It was touch and go, but as of now, yes."

"Thank God. Why didn't you call earlier?"

"I couldn't get them to give me information. Those motherfuckers insisted that they could only talk to family. I'm now family."

"Explain."

"I'm Beth's fiancé."

"We're going to talk about that, but first tell me how she's doing."

"She was bit five hours ago. It was a rattlesnake. I sucked out most of the venom, but it struck on her thigh near her femoral artery, but some of the poison got into her blood supply. It was touch and go. Now they're worried about possible paralysis."

"Fuck. That girl doesn't deserve this. Thank God you were there Preston."

"I should have been right by her side. I let her pick flowers in the field by herself. I should have been by her side." Jack's voice broke.

"Jack, it sounds like she's going to live because of your quick action."

"Clint, I can handle anything. I'm a SEAL. I've had team mates die. But I...I..."

"What hospital are you at?" Clint got a pen and was ready to write down the information.

"You know you can't come. We need to keep the sisters apart. She's going to live. If Beth needs Lydia, I'd tell you. Right now we're keeping to her cover story. She's Beth Ochoa, and she's staying with me and my family at the ranch."

"And the fiancé business?" But Clint knew. He didn't

need Jack to tell him. Beth had captured the man's heart as surely as Lydia had captured his.

"Right now I said it to get the hospital to give me information. I went crazy when I didn't know what was going on. But Clint, I have deep feelings for Beth. She doesn't realize it. She's still fragile. I'm taking this slow. But nothing will stop me from keeping her safe."

"What if she needs to be protected from you, Jack?"

"Then I will do that too. I will never, ever harm Beth." Jack's sincerity came through loud and clear.

"How soon before you can arrange for Lydia to talk to Beth?"

"Probably the day after tomorrow. Everything they told me is she is going to be out of it until then."

"Lydia will want to talk to you. She won't want this information second hand."

"Not a problem."

"Is there anyone else at the hospital with you?"

"Yes. My mom and my stepdad are here." Clint smiled. It was good Jack had the emotional support.

"Expect a call later tonight or tomorrow morning first thing."

"Okay."

"And Jack?"

"Yes."

"Thank you for saving Beth's life."

Clint set down the phone and went in to check on Lydia. She was sleeping deeply. She was going to kill him in the morning, she would say she should have been told immediately. But to what purpose? She could sleep and face this situation with more strength in the morning. She was going to skin him alive in the morning.

IT WAS SO MUCH WORSE than he ever imagined. He would have embraced her anger, but her fear and anguish were ripping him apart.

"Did you see her?" Lydia didn't even realize she was crying. She was staring at the blank computer screen where Beth's ravaged face had just been. Jack smuggled his phone into the hospital room to do a skype call, but Beth had barely been aware of Lydia's voice.

"I saw her baby."

"Would you hold me?" She was already seated next to him on the sofa, his arm around her shoulders, but it obviously wasn't registering.

"Always." He picked her up and cradled her in his arms. Sobs started in earnest.

"She could have died. My baby sister could have died."

"But she didn't." Lydia just cried harder. Clint was at a loss, so he just started to rock her. Finally, she hiccupped and shuddered. She tried to get off his lap.

"What do you need?"

"Kleenex." He settled her on the couch and brought the roll of paper towels to her.

"We can't go to her, can we?" Clint sat down and arranged her so she was snuggled close again.

"No baby we can't."

"Jack said they're worried about paralysis." She pushed her face against the crook of his neck and he hugged her tighter. He didn't say anything.

"Partial paralysis. They already know she can move her arms and legs honey. They're talking about maybe having to use a walker." Her nails dug into his back.

"Let's not borrow trouble. As soon as she's really conscious they'll know. Jack will call us."

"I'm so glad Jack didn't tell Mama and Papa. They're too fragile right now. After we know what the prognosis is, then they can be told."

"That's why he asked you. We both thought you would know best."

"When will this be over?"

"Soon baby. Soon." Clint held her while she stared at the blank computer screen until she fell into a restless sleep.

LYDIA STARED out the sliding glass door at the steady stream of rain. She'd left the warm bed and an even warmer Clint. He'd crawled in much later than she did, so he should sleep through until morning. God, she loved that man. Clint Archer.

She watched the rain splatter on the wood of the balcony, she could see the individual raindrops. Lydia remembered being wrapped close in Clint's arms in the jungle and seeing raindrops on the leaves. She'd been so sick and in so much pain, but that was when she truly started falling in love.

For five days, Clint carried her in his arms, and even with all of the pain and fear, she felt cherished. She breathed hot air on the glass, and then drew a heart in the fogged glass. The man had her heart.

Just two more weeks and her father would testify. Mason said they might be able to get one of Guzman's men to talk. She'd hear about Beth's condition tomorrow. No wonder she was up in the middle of the night. Right now it just seemed like everything was on a precipice. It was a night for dreams. She would really get to meet Clint's family. They would get to build a life together.

She winced thinking such happy thoughts when Beth's condition was so dire. She rested her forehead against the cold glass.

"Hey beautiful, couldn't sleep?" Clint's arms wrapped around her waist. She leaned back against him.

"Now I'm feeling a little bit of déjà vu. Didn't we just do this?"

"Yeah we did. Where's my cocoa?" He kissed the side of her face and she smiled.

"It's all catching up with me. I was actually thinking some good thoughts and then I felt guilty."

"Beth?"

"Yes." She nuzzled her head against his chin.

"At three p.m. our time we'll know her prognosis." He rubbed her arms in comfort.

"I'm going to go crazy until then." He turned her around so he could tip her chin up and place a soft kiss on her lips. He looked deep in her eyes.

"I know what we could do to pass the time." Lydia kept a smile on her face. She didn't want to make love, and was hurt he thought she would.

"I think it's time for a marathon game of *League of Legends*," he continued.

Life sparkled. The man was perfect.

"Get the computers booted up. I know you know my password. I'll go start some hot chocolate." He let her go and went to the computers.

"I want Mountain Dew and some Doritos."

"You are such a teenage boy." She giggled as she went to the kitchen.

MASON CALLED an hour before they were supposed to hear from Jack.

"I've got good news and I've got bad news."

"I want the good news first," Clint said as he looked at his Lieutenant on the video call. Mason looked dead on his feet. Drake was beside him. Both of them looked like they hadn't had slept for days.

"One of Guzman's men rolled."

"That's great!" Lydia exclaimed. Clint had his arm around her as they sat on the couch watching the computer screen. He knew the bad news was going to undo the good news.

"Yep. It looks like a pretty straight line. Guzman's drug trade has been suffering as the US Border patrol picked up. It turns out one of Guzman's legitimate businesses was in the US and was a big contributor the Congressman's re-election campaign and s why he was voting against the increase in Border Patrol funding. The DEA agents knew this because Guzman was also using one of the DEA agents your Dad is testifying against to provide fun-money."

"I don't get it, why not just set up an account and wire transfers." Lydia asked.

"The congressman was worried those could get traced. Also, he wanted some fun cocaine to go with the fun money."

"Jesus. He's just all kinds of wrong," Clint bit out. "So this sounds like great news. We have this idiot's testimony against the DEA agent, the Congressman and against Guzman. Plus, you stopped four months of supply with that bust. It sounds like great fucking news to me. What's the bad news?"

"We found eight young women with the drug bust. Five Hispanic, three from Asia. They were all set to be going to the US as well. Nobody will tell us dick about them. Looks like Guzman started a new business endeavor."

"Human trafficking?" Lydia was aghast.

"It was bad, Lydia." Drake answered. "When we questioned the girls, we found out that there were many more they'd been separated from. That's why you've been seeing all that information on the net about Guzman selling his drug product so much faster than normal. He needed it to start up this new business." Drake looked sick.

"The bastard!"

"That's probably why he needed the Congressman to loosen up the border, not so much for the drugs, but for the slave trade," Clint said.

"Don't call them slaves," Drake spit out.

"I'm sorry man," Clint apologized.

"One of the girls told us something we're following up on. It sounds like Berto is liking to get up and personal with the only certain specific Hispanic girls as they're brought in. Give us another couple of days."

"If you get Berto there's a real possibility he'll give you his father. Berto is a spoiled piece of trash who would do anything to save his own skin," Lydia told Drake and Mason.

"Are you sure Lydia? He would turn in his own father?" Mason asked, giving her a considering look.

"There used to be another Guzman brother. Alfonso Jr. was Berto's older brother. He died under suspicious circumstances. Rumor has it Berto had him killed so he could move up in the family business. So yeah, I definitely think he would turn on *Daddy Dearest* if it would benefit him."

"Got it. Okay, I need to work with some of my overseas contacts about the human trafficking angle. This just makes me sick."

Lydia re-evaluated her original estimation of Drake and Mason's condition. Maybe they weren't tired from having been up for a long time, maybe their hearts were tired.

The men broke the connection, and then it was time for their call with Jack. He got on the computer screen and he had a huge grin on his face. Just like that, the previous conversation was forgotten.

"She's going to make a total recovery."

"When can I talk to her?"

"Maybe tonight. Probably tomorrow. Lydia, she's going to be fine!" Jack looked every bit as worn out as Drake and Mason had. He had a couple of days of beard growth, his short hair hadn't seen a comb in days. There were dark circles under his eyes, but his smile lit up the screen. It suddenly occurred to Lydia this man was a lot more attached to her sister than a mere bodyguard.

"I will never be able to thank you enough for saving her life, Jack."

"I'm just thankful she's okay," he said fervently.

"After I talk to her, I'll call my parents."

"Good, I was going to ask you if you could. I figured it would be best if the news could come from you." Jack yawned.

"We'll let you go. It looks like you could use some shut eye, man. I'm with Lydia, I can't thank you enough for your quick thinking." Jack looked uncomfortable with the praise from his fellow SEAL.

"Thanks, Clint. You're right, I need to get some rest. I'll call you back as soon as she can take a call."

As soon as Jack disconnected, Lydia threw her arms around Clint's neck. She didn't say a word, she just pressed as close as she could, and she was panting.

He burrowed his hand under her hair and pulled her back slightly so he could see her face.

"Baby, are you okay?" She was flushed, her gaze took him a moment to read. Finally, he saw passion and greed.

"I need you."

"Whatever you want, I'm here."

IT HAD all been too much. Everything just piled on top of one another for the last twenty-four hours. Lydia felt like she'd been caught up in a tornado, her emotions spun out of control. Even now that things seemed to be good, she couldn't settle. She was coming out of her skin. She needed.

She felt a little bad. She wasn't looking at Clint like the man she loved, she was looking at him as a man she wanted to ravish, to fuck. Those shoulders, that face. His eyes glittered, there was a flush on his high cheekbones. She looked downwards and saw his erection pushing against his jeans. Thank God! He was wanted her too.

She knelt down.

"Baby no."

"Yes," she snarled at him, and wondered if she looked frantic or fierce. She unbuttoned his jeans, then thought left her head as she looked at the beauty of his cock. She needed. He stripped off his jeans.

"Your shirt, I need to see all of you. Now!" He yanked it over his head and she stared at his naked beauty. She then looked down at erect flesh and wrapped her hand around him. He barely gave her time to stroke and lick, before he lifted her up to the couch.

"You're in a mood Lydia."

She pushed at his chest. "I can't explain it. It's like every one of my nerve endings are on the outside. I'm overwhelmed and the only thing I know that will make it better is having you inside me. Fast. Hard. Deep." He shuddered.

"Now you've done it." His hand went to her blouse and yanked. Buttons pinged across the room. Something settled inside her. She shrugged, helping him to get her out of the shirt. They both worked on the bra, and it was tossed aside too. Her jeans and panties followed.

Clint grabbed for his jeans and found a condom, as she bit his shoulder hard to reprimand him for taking so long.

"Sorry," he groaned as he sheathed himself. He started to slide his hand down her torso. She knew he was going to make sure she was aroused enough to take him.

"Fuck me now," she growled at him, her face a tight mask of need.

"Never. I will always take care of you." He brushed his fingers gently against her. She knew she was wild, wet and wanton. She wrapped both legs around his hips and surged upwards.

He plunged deep and she gave a wail of satisfaction. Perfection. But...

"Are you okay, Clint?"

"Are you kidding? Shut up and kiss me. I'm in heaven."

No, *she* was in heaven, and she had a warrior angel of old, giving her a guided tour.

"WAKE UP, BABY."

"Don't wanna." Lydia burrowed deeper into the pillow that smelled like Clint.

"It's important."

"Then I really don' wanna." She sounded petulant, but she didn't care. She peeked at the clock on the nightstand it was three in the morning. He was being all whispery soft and kind. It might be 'important', but it wasn't urgent. She wanted a few more moments in bed before she had to face reality.

He brushed back her hair and kissed her neck. Then he licked. Then he blew.

She sat up. "That's cold," she said as she pushed at him.

"Got you moving, though." She grabbed his pillow, and pulled it to her breast, and stared at him.

"So what's so important?"

"The team will be here soon."

"Not Mason," she wailed. "It's Sophia's birthday tomorrow."

"Don't worry, baby, he's joining us via Skype." She rubbed her chin into the top of the pillow.

"Okay, when will they be here?"

"They were down in the lobby. They're probably cooling their heels outside our door as we speak."

"Go let them in."

"Don't be walking around just wearing a blanket. Real clothes this time."

"Who knew you'd be such a prude." She watched as he left. Lydia wondered why Drake and Darius were here. She wanted a few more minutes of not knowing. Was that too much to ask for?

All three men were standing around the seating area. Darius and Drake were tense, they had obviously been waiting for her.

"What's up?" She looked over at Clint and he shrugged. He held out his hand and she went to him.

"Let's get Mason on the video," Drake suggested. Darius was already starting the call. Drake wouldn't look her in the eye.

"Drake, what's up?" She insisted.

"One time, Lydia, I just want this said one time. If we're wrong, we'll never mention it again, you have my word." She got a really bad feeling as Drake looked down at her, his eyes soft with sympathy.

"Hi, guys," Mason said from the computer screen.

"Lieutenant, you're scaring my best girl. Let's cut to the chase."

"We got some information on Berto. Well, on all the Guzman's." Mason looked directly at her. His eyes were piercing and sympathetic. Damn, she was scared.

"Is it my parents?"

"Your family is fine for now. We're trying to put some of the puzzle pieces together. After your Dad started working for the accounting firm, did you ever meet Guzman or his sons?"

"No!"

"Think Lydia, you were pretty young when he went to work for him."

Lydia leaned over the table where the computer was placed, so she could get into Mason's face. "Mason, I've been tracking this asshole for almost two years now, I'd remember him or his spawns."

"Okay, we didn't think so. Do you think Beth has?"

"No."

Mason just looked at her. All of the other men in the room were silent.

"I said 'no'."

"Baby, how would you know if Beth had or hadn't met them?" Clint asked.

"She would have told me."

"Lydia, did your dad ever take Beth to his office?" This time it was Darius asking. Lydia plopped down on the couch.

"I don't understand. Why would it matter if she had met them? It would have been a long time ago. What's this all about?"

"It matters because Berto is fucking nuts. That's why." Drake just sounded defeated. He wasn't yelling, he wasn't sounding outraged. Now she was *really* scared.

"Please, won't one of you tell me what is going on? Is Beth in some sort of danger? I mean besides the obvious of having to hide from killers?" Clint sat down next to her on the couch, and turned the laptop so it was facing the two of them. Darius and Drake sat on either side of them. It was a tight squeeze, but they all managed to fit, so Mason could see them.

"Please Mason, talk to me. Don't make me wait." Drake patted her hand, as if to tell her it would be all right.

"He's not trying to drag this out. He needed you to answer those questions, honey."

"Lydia," Mason began, "we got our information on Berto's obsession with the certain types of women. Remember when we told you that he only wanted to *interact* with a specific type of Hispanic woman?"

"Cut the euphemisms Mason. I remember perfectly. Of the Hispanic and Asian women, he planned to sell, he would rape the Hispanic women, but only certain ones. Yeah, got that the first time. It still makes me sick to think about it." Lydia tried to keep her shit together but it was getting tougher.

"Lydia, one of the guys who started talking said something pretty interesting. He said Berto was the one who was going to come witness your family's murder at the shack. He told everyone Beth wasn't to be harmed, and she would be leaving with him."

"But he doesn't know Beth. It doesn't make any sense. But I thank God for it. Her life would have been spared." She clapped her hand over her mouth. Her eyes widened in horror. Beth wouldn't have been spared. What unimaginable things would have happened to her?

"Mason, what else did this guy say?" Clint asked.

"He knew nothing more than that when it came to Beth, but that scared the hell out of us. It means Berto has targeted her. All we can figure is somewhere down the line he's met her. Lydia, we're going to have to ask your dad."

"This is going to kill Papa." She pressed close to Clint's warmth. "He's going to hate himself for putting Beth at risk, but there is no other explanation."

"We do have good news. The same guy had a lot to say about daddy Guzman. He gave up everything. Shit, he even drew maps to guide the Mexican authorities to Guzman's plantations. His operation is shut down.

Tomorrow, they're going to raid the place where he should be and arrest him."

"Thank God."

"It's possible after tomorrow's arrest, we'll have all the evidence we need against the congressman. It might mean Guzman's drug empire is no more. If that really happens, then the reprisals that the US Marshall's have been worried about, are gone. You and your family won't have to go into Witness Protection."

"What about Berto and his sick fascination with Beth?"

"He didn't have any idea of his whereabouts. But we should be able to find him. Everyone involved is hell-bent on taking down the human trafficking ring. We're sure there will be some evidence when they capture Guzman tomorrow. Until we do, you and your parents might not have to be under guard, but your sister will be."

"That doesn't make any fucking sense," Clint ground out. "Won't Berto be likely to seek retribution on the rest of the Hidalgo family?"

"No," Lydia said tiredly. "I know him. He's not his father. He's not some cartel crime lord. You know this Clint. You've read the same things I have. He's all about Berto and making money. If he's moved onto human trafficking, he's just in it for the money. And apparently my sister," Lydia's voice broke.

"We're going to get him, there is no fucking way this fucking bastard will get his fucking hands on Beth." Drake stood up and started pacing the length of the hotel suite.

"But I wanted this to be over with, for everyone." Lydia pressed the heel of her hand to her eyes. She felt a headache coming on. Clint squeezed the back of her neck, offering relief.

"So now we wait. When is the raid going down?" Clint asked.

"Three o'clock."

"Will Mama and Papa still have to be in protective custody until the trial?"

Mason traded glances with Darius and Clint who were still sitting on the couch. "It's probably for the best, Lydia. The DEA agents are out on bail."

"Okay." She wanted to go back to bed. "Oh yeah, I hope you have a nice time with Sophia. She deserves a great birthday. Clint told me about all she's been through."

"We have quite the party planned. Hopefully you'll get to meet her soon."

"That'd be nice Mason. Really nice." She rubbed her temple. Her head was really beginning to pound.

"Okay, let's wrap this up. I need to get Lydia some aspirin and back to bed."

"Good night, Lydia. Guys, I'll keep you informed." Mason signed off.

Darius stood and joined Drake at the door of the suite.

"Call us when you get up. Lydia, I hope you get to feeling better," Drake said as he walked out the door.

She slumped against the back of the couch. The next thing she knew Clint was giving her some water and two white tablets.

"Here, Baby." She swallowed.

"Sorry," she said looking up at him. Damn the light was hurting her eyes. She closed them. He picked her up and carried her to their bedroom. He helped her out of her clothes and she lay there with him. The pain didn't subside and she whimpered.

"Let me work on you. You're tensing up and the pain's getting worse, isn't it?"

"Yes," her voice was slurred.

Clint gently rolled her over. He pushed her hair over her head and did a couple of soft touches up and down her back and then lightly stroked her neck and scalp. She pushed up into his fingers trying to increase the pressure.

"Don't move baby, I'll do it harder." Over time his touch became more firm, until she finally sighed in relief.

"You can stop now. I feel better."

"Just go to sleep. I like touching you."

She drifted off with the feel of Clint caressing and caring for her.

11

"I want to talk about Rylie." Were the first words out of Darius' mouth as he entered the hotel suite. Thank God she was firing on all cylinders; otherwise Lydia didn't think she would have been able to have handled such an abrupt change in topic from last night's.

"Okay," she said slowly. "What do you want to talk about?"

"Has she contacted you? What have you been doing to find her? Is she still messed up with this Guzman shit?"

"Whoa there Hoss. Let's order up some breakfast. Lydia hasn't even had her coffee. We'll tell you everything we know." Clint clamped a hand on his friend's shoulder and guided him towards the dining room table where the coffee pot sat. Lydia gave Drake a questioning look, and he just shook his head in confusion.

Darius poured himself some coffee. All three men took it black, while Lydia doctored hers up with an appropriate amount of cream and sugar.

"The last time Rylie contacted us we tracked her down to Oklahoma," Clint said.

"Where?"

"We don't know."

"Why not?"

Darius was asking the questions rapid fire. Clint was showing a hell of a lot more patience than she would have been. What the hell was Darius' problem?

"Look, Darius," Lydia interrupted. "Rylie has been on the net as Sylvia for over three years. I'm betting that before then she was doing a hell of a lot under different names. She is one of the best I've ever run into."

"So she's wily, like a coyote," Drake chimed in. He laughed at his own joke. Everyone scowled at him.

"What I'm saying Darius is that we were lucky to track her to Oklahoma. We've been concentrating on the Guzman case, and now I want to nail Berto, but finding Rylie is important, so we won't give up on her."

"You don't understand." Darius hadn't touched his coffee, he looked between Clint and Lydia. "She's young, her parents are dead, she's been abused and she doesn't have an anchor. She's going to keep taking risks until something bad happens to her because she thinks this Robin Hood thing is her only purpose. She has no sense of self-preservation. We've got to stop her."

"You can't know that," Drake said.

"Yes I can." His teeth were clenched. The last time she had seen him look like that was when he had been ministering to her in the jungle.

"Explain it to us, Darius. Tell us how you know this," she said gently. She reached over the table and grabbed his clenched fist.

"I grew up in foster care. I just know." He looked her dead in the eye, ignoring Clint and Drake. "I know."

"Then it's a done deal," Drake said. "As soon as

Guzman is handled, we have two number one priorities. We find the fucker Berto, and we make sure Rylie is cared for." Darius pulled his hand away from Lydia and picked up his coffee.

"All right then."

"I want breakfast. Does this place serve grits, or is it too hoity-toity?" Clint called in the room service order, and Drake bitched all during breakfast that they didn't have grits on the menu.

Darius got up first from the table. Lydia watched as he went to the window to look outside. He then came back to the table and sat down. Two minutes later Drake repeated the process. When Clint did the same thing, curiosity got to her.

"What is going on? Are you worried someone is going to come here?" Clint looked over at her with a rueful expression.

"We're just antsy, Baby. We can't stand the thought of Mason and the others in harm's way in Mexico and us sitting here. So we're just walking around and looking for shadows."

"Enough already." Drake went to his jacket and pulled out a dog-eared deck of cards. "Clint, see if you can at least get some GPS going on the team, and track them. In the meantime, let's see if we can settle by playing a little poker."

Clint pulled up his computer and soon they had Mason's position pinpointed. He wasn't moving.

"I'm going to set it up so it pings as soon as he moves. In the meantime, I intend to win back all the cash that I lost to Darius last time."

"Dream on, buddy. I'm the master at poker." Lydia listened to the byplay. She'd only played poker once, but she remembered the rules, they seemed straightforward enough.

"Deal me in."

It took over an hour before the computer pinged to let them know Mason was on the move. Nobody was really interested in the game, and stopped playing to watch the computer screen.

"There!" Drake pointed to a building. "That's their target. It's acquired." Lydia watched as all the men seemed to hold their collective breaths when Mason's dot stopped moving on the screen. They let it out as one when it started to move again.

"Does Mason know you can track him?" Lydia asked.

"Clint tracks everyone," Drake answered. "All of our cells have tracking devices for Clint to follow us. I'm sure Clint doctored the burner phone you got so he could track you."

"Did you?"

"Hell yes." For some reason that made her feel comforted.

The icon for Mason stopped again.

Clint got a text.

"They got him!" Mason said he'd SKYPE with us when he could. The relief in the suite was palpable. They went back to playing cards, and Darius beat everyone easily. Two hours later Mason was on the screen. He spoke directly to Lydia.

"They got him, Lydia. Guzman is in custody. Everything went down without a hitch."

"What about Berto?"

"What we're being told is it's going to take a couple of days to sort through everything to find any evidence of Berto and the human trafficking ring."

"So Guzman didn't say anything?" Clint asked.

"I'm sorry man. No he didn't. They have him in for questioning. I spoke to Inspector Rios and he's sure he can get him to talk."

"He won't," Lydia said dejectedly.

"I agree," Mason said. "We're really counting on finding something on his computers. I was told he had quite the set-up. In the meantime, your sister is safe in hiding. Once Berto is captured, your whole family will be able to live a life without fear of reprisal from Guzman. But..."

"But what?"

"I talked to Rios. He didn't think it was ever really going to be safe for your father to come back to Mexico City. Even with Guzman out of the picture, there are going to be too many people who will remember him."

Lydia nodded.

"CLINT, I don't know what to do," Lydia whispered.

She was sitting cross legged in the middle of the bed, staring at her laptop. "How do I tell my parents the great news that they'll be free when the trial is over, but Beth still has to remain in hiding because a madman is after her? How do I tell Beth?"

She rocked back and forth, tapping on the space bar.

"Lydia, you don't have to tell them anything right now. Everything is status quo. They all have to stay under protection until after the trial anyway. Why confront this?" *Dammit, why did everything always fall on Lydia's shoulders?*

"Because it's the right thing to do."

"Why? What's it going to accomplish? You tell them, they stay where they are. You don't tell them. They stay where they are." She looked up at him.

"That's true, isn't it?" She looked so hopeful.

"What's more, you know everyone is looking for Berto Guzman. By the time the trial is over with, that asshole will probably be in custody so it will be a moot point." Lydia stopped tapping and rocking.

"We're going to help find that asshole. We've got a week until Papa has to testify. You're right, this is nothing. We brought down an international drug cartel! We can stop his slime ball son!"

Clint gave her a big grin. He didn't want to do anything to diminish her enthusiasm. But he'd talked to Mason and he knew they were fighting an uphill battle. Still if anyone deserved some luck, it was the Hidalgo sisters.

"Okay Lydia. Let's blow this Popsicle stand and get something to eat. I'm sick of room service. We can work out some strategy over dinner. How does that sound." She snapped shut her laptop and jumped off the bed.

"That sounds wonderful. Just give me a quick second to change. Are the guys coming with us?"

"No, they needed some downtime. It'll just be the two of us. I would expect to see Darius first thing tomorrow morning. This thing with Rylie really has him rattled."

"They're just really giving me space, aren't they?" she said as she went to the closet.

"Does it matter?" he asked as he watched her pull out a blue dress.

"No. I guess it doesn't."

"After dinner, let's call Melvin. Maybe he knows something he doesn't even know he knows about Rylie."

"Damn, Lydia, that even kind of made sense." She

grinned over her shoulder as she closed the door to the bathroom.

"How often do you and Mr. Muscles have sex anyway?" Melvin asked. Lydia and Clint were on the living room couch listening to Melvin on the speakers of the computer.

"What?" Lydia was taken aback by the question, and luckily Clint stepped in.

"Baby, he basically wants to know when you're going to want to video Skype with him again. Which will be never," Clint said into the computer speaker.

"Damn, he has a brain too?"

"Did I tell you he's a Navy SEAL?" Lydia asked sweetly.

"Please say you're kidding me." Melvin sounded like he was in pain.

"She's just pulling your leg, Melvin."

There was a long silence.

"Melvin? Are you there?" Lydia asked.

"Hold on, Kitten. I need just a little bit longer." Clint held up his can of Mountain Dew to see if she wanted a sip, she shuddered as she shook her head. She did steal some Doritos out of his bag on the coffee table.

"Senior Chief Petty Officer Clint Archer, stationed out of San Diego. You're originally from Denver. Your middle name is Anthony. You really are a fucking Navy SEAL and I'm never going to be able to video SKYPE with Lydia again, am I?" Melvin sounded dejected.

"Nope, you won't. On the plus side, you've made some strong allies."

"I'm not sure that makes up for the loss of seeing her in an angora sweater."

Lydia squirmed.

"You own an angora sweater?" Clint asked, the Dorito halfway to his mouth.

"Enough guys. This is important." *Seriously, men and boobs. Why women didn't rule the world was beyond her.*

"Melvin, did you hear Guzman was arrested today?"

"It was damn near all anyone talked about today. It made the dark net headlines." Melvin laughed at his joke.

"I have two problems. Berto is on the loose and he doesn't seem to care about the drug business imploding. He's onto a new business," Lydia explained.

"Yep, that made page two. He's now in the sex slave business."

"Melvin, can you please say human trafficking."

"I believe in calling it the way it is," he protested.

"Well then, let me inform you, that seventeen percent of the people sold into the US are sold for labor, not sexual slavery. So human trafficking is more accurate. I abhor that term." She'd agreed with Drake, and was grateful when he had made a point to have the team stop using the phrase. The least she could do is follow through with others.

"I'm going to check your stats, but you're right, I should be more respectful. Now that we're done with the PC version of our program, tell me what you need from me."

"I need any and all information on Berto. But just as critical I need any and all information on Sylvia Hessman and someone named Rylie Jones."

"Ahhh, you figured that one out, did you."

"You knew?"

"Yeah, since last year. I did some digging. I hate not knowing about my associates. It was odd to find out I was swapping information with a dead girl. But believe it or not she's not my most interesting contact. There's this guy from New Jersey who's trying to get into the Guinness Book of World Records for speaking entirely in Klingon for the longest amount of time. He only has five more months and he'll make the book."

"Klingon?" Lydia asked.

"That's a fake language from the television show Star Trek," Clint answered.

"Not fake my friend. It has been made into a full-fledged language."

"Clint, didn't you hear? In order for this man from New Jersey has to beat out somebody else, he has to continue speaking Klingon for five more months." Lydia put her hand over her mouth to stop the little giggle. But then it became a bigger giggle. Then it was a chuckle. Then it was a full blown laugh and she couldn't stop it from bursting forth.

"Melvin, that's wonderful! You have the best contacts in the world. Oh my God. This is too funny."

Clint and Melvin were laughing as well.

"Yeah well, at least he's allowed to type in English."

"Okay, back to the reason for our call," Clint said.

"I can definitely help with Berto, but you need to tell me why you want the info on Rylie."

"Melvin, that's why I love working with you. You're loyal to a fault," Lydia stated. "I'm really worried about her. She's been getting pretty scary information and now she's dropped from the grid."

"She's twelve. She needs some people in her life

helping her," Clint interrupted. Lydia elbowed him in his ribs.

"Clint, she might look twelve, but I believe the girl I investigated was twenty-one," Melvin said wryly.

"You're right," Lydia agreed. "But we met her. Rylie or Sylvia or whatever you want to call her is a force to be reckoned with. I was really impressed by her. But she was awfully alone. I think she could use some help."

Again they were met by silence. Finally, Melvin sighed. "Lydia, it's all that testosterone isn't it. They can't help themselves."

Lydia laughed. "That's definitely part of it, put a bunch of them together and they start with the cavemen tactics."

"Okay, I'll start putting together everything I can on Rylie. To tell you the truth, I've been worried about her myself. Hey, I've got to go." Melvin was gone.

"That was fast, was he upset?" Clint asked.

"Nah," Lydia said as she went to get something decent to drink out of the hotel's little refrigerator. "He probably had somebody else pinging him." She grabbed the lemonade and poured herself a glass. She went back and settled onto the couch.

"Now I have one important question to ask you, Lydia." Uh-oh, he sounded so serious.

"Okay." She set down her lemonade, uncaring that it might leave a stain on the wood.

"Did you pack the angora sweater?"

"YOU TWO SURE look chipper this morning," Drake noted as he plowed into his omelet.

Clint eyed his two friends who arrived for breakfast a

half hour ago. Darius was barely eating, which went against all of their training. You always took in food when it was available. Rylie had him tied up in knots, and he didn't think it was just the foster kid connection. Darius looked up.

"Got something to say, Archer?"

"Nope, just enjoying my breakfast. Shouldn't you be?"

"Not hungry. You know we have to leave this afternoon. I was hoping for an update." Clint sighed inwardly, and then Lydia spoke up.

"Some info came in while Clint was in the shower. You know we figure she lives in Oklahoma because we tracked her to that Internet Provider. There have been some awfully large donations that have been happening for the last two years to a home for abused and neglected children in Fallon Springs, OK. The donations have been anonymous wire transfers. Over a half million."

Drake whistled.

"The home went under investigation because of the money last year. Then miraculously the donor came to light. It all came from this old man in North Carolina who was known to contribute generously to charities. It stopped the investigation in its tracks. But when Melvin dug a little further he found that Mr. Curruthers had been in a nursing home for dementia for the last two years. It couldn't have been him."

"Okay, what is the name of this place in Fallon Springs?" Darius asked.

"Forever After. And before you ask Darius. I've checked the records of all the staff, Rylie doesn't work there."

"But it's a damn good lead." Darius smiled. "Who the hell is this guy Melvin?"

"Don't ask. Lydia has the most eclectic group of friends you could ever imagine. Anyway, we'll keep at this. One more thing to consider, Dare."

"What?"

"Your girl has an anchor. This place, Forever After, is an anchor. She has ties to it, it's someplace she wants to help and make a difference for."

Darius considered his words and finally nodded. He started to eat the food in front of him.

Clint reached over and stroked Lydia's hair, before grabbing her hand and kissing it.

They'd started making good headway on one of their priorities, he just wished they had some kind of lead on the second. Only he didn't think the problem with Berto was going to be as easily solved.

"Lydia, I'm going to drive the guys to the airport this afternoon, is that okay?"

"Okay, I can also check a couple of other sources. I also want to start packing."

"Hey man, we can catch a shuttle," Drake said. Clint just raised his eyebrow and Drake shut up.

"Okay, what did you need to talk to us about without Lydia hearing?" Drake asked as he threw his duffle into the trunk of the rental car.

"Remember what we pulled off for Mason when he proposed to Sophia."

"Oh hell no, you are not going to copy what Mason did! That is such a craptastic idea. Lydia finds out you did that and she'll divorce your ass. Women talk."

"Jesus, Drake, give me more credit than that." Clint said as he got behind the wheel.

"No, I just meant I needed to pull off something. When I proposed I didn't even have a ring. I need to pull out all the stops when we get to San Diego, and I'm going to be counting on you guys to help me."

"You got it. What do you have in mind?" Drake asked.

"A couple of things. First and foremost is getting all of the Hidalgos to San Diego after the trial. I don't care if Berto is still out there, I want Beth there. I want this to be a big surprise engagement party for Lydia. She hasn't seen her family for a long time."

"Gotchya."

"Have any of you talked to Jack Preston?"

"Not since he was assigned to Beth," Darius answered. "I know Finn has been keeping in touch, because I've been talking to Finn a lot. He's been having me keep an eye on his mom."

"Hey, why didn't he ask me to keep an eye on her?" Drake protested.

"Mellow," Darius said soothingly. "Finn knew if he asked you, you would have smothered her."

"I would not have."

"Yes you would have. I've been checking in on her twice a week."

"Only twice a week? What the hell man? She's a widow! Her dad just died. Finn just uprooted her from Minnesota to San Diego and then left on assignment. You can't just let her fend for herself. You needed to be seeing her a hell of a lot more often than twice a week!"

Darius didn't say anything and Clint just concentrated on driving.

"Dare, are you listening to me?" Drake demanded.

Neither of them responded.

"Did you hear me?"

"Like I said Drake, you would have smothered her." Darius sighed. "So Clint, I talked to Finn, it sounds like Jack might have taken a shine to Beth."

"Yeah, something is definitely brewing. You heard she was in the hospital, right?" Clint asked.

"Yeah, Finn told me."

"What the fuck, you never told me that!" Drake spun around in the passenger seat to glare at Darius in the back seat.

"Shit Drake, I'm sorry. Yeah, Beth was bit by a rattler, and it was touch and go. I didn't hear until days later."

"Anyway, I talked to Jack five hours after it happened," Clint explained. "He was a basket case. I thought he would lose his shit. I just want to see how Beth is handling things with him. It will be good to see them together. We're going to need a boatload of security unless we get Berto before then."

"It's possible we will find him," Drake said in a hopeful tone, but he was aware of the truth, just like Clint. Berto was in the wind.

"Even if we don't find him, we've got Beth covered. So when are you thinking for the shindig? Do you want to do this all elegant, rent out a room at a restaurant?" Darius questioned.

"Fuck that shit. I know the perfect thing." Drake got out his phone and made a call. Clint listened and smiled. Drake was right, it *was* perfect.

12

"LYDIA, I NEED YOU IN THE LIVING ROOM. WE HAVE A problem." Clint yelled from outside the bathroom door. She put down the mascara and willed herself to be calm. If something happened to her family Clint would not have sounded like that. This was just another problem. *You can cope girl.*

Clint was in front of his computer talking to someone. As she got closer she could hear Mason's voice.

"Why didn't you call me first lieutenant?" Oh shit, Clint was pissed. He never called Mason by his rank.

"Because I didn't want you to have to lie to Jack. I wanted to be the one to have to do it."

Lydia came up behind Clint and looked over his shoulder. "Why did you have to lie to Jack?" Clint asked.

"It just pinged today that Beth Hidalgo was in the hospital in San Antonio, not Beth Ochoa. Beth's cover has been blown."

"Oh no. They've got to get out of there. Do you think they'll figure out she's at Jack's ranch?" Lydia asked.

"It's likely. Jack told everyone he was her fiancé. She has to get the hell out of San Antonio. I told him you wanted Beth to come stay with the two of you but that I said no," Mason said.

"Why the fuck would you have said 'no'?" Clint asked. "Beth staying with us would be perfect. With Berto after her, I can protect her. We're going to be in San Diego tomorrow."

"Think Clint, you haven't told her about Berto have you? She still thinks that Guzman is out there after her whole family."

"Fuck. You're right. The whole idea is that the sisters need to be kept apart. Fuck me." Clint nodded.

"This is my fault. I'll call Beth right now and explain what I should have as soon as Guzman was captured. I'll tell her about Berto and everything."

"Hold up Lydia," Mason said. "Another thing you need to know is I told Jack that I would be re-assigning Beth to someone else, and he basically told me it would be over his dead body." Lydia felt her heart grow lighter.

"That's a good thing Mason. From the conversations I've had with Beth, I think it would break her heart if they were parted."

"Okay Mason, now that we know everything, what are you thinking we should do?"

"I think we should have Beth and Jack go undercover to Los Angeles. It's close enough to San Diego and we can we can provide a rotation of people to help Jack out so he has plenty of back-up. It's big enough that even the natives get lost, and Lydia and her parents will be close by."

"When do I tell her about Berto?"

"We still don't need to baby. Until the trial we still have

time to find Berto without having to tell her or your parents, it's still status quo. The day after your father testifies and he doesn't have to go into the Witness Protection Program, then we have to tell them about Guzman being in custody, but Berto trying to kidnap your sister."

"What a tangled web we weave, once we practice to deceive." Lydia sighed out a deep breath. "Okay, I agree."

"Mason, thanks for keeping us informed. Can you work out the details with Jack? I need to talk to Lydia."

"Sure."

The screen went blank.

"Hey lady, come here." Clint reached around the back of the chair and pulled her down onto his lap. "What's going on?"

"What do you mean?" Lydia sank into his warmth, allowing him to comfort her. He pulled her tighter and tilted up her chin so that their eyes met.

"I mean that shit about the tangled web. You haven't been lying to your family. You just haven't told them something that would scare the hell out of them. Especially Beth. You know how vulnerable she is, and this is something that is going to really be difficult for her."

"I know. I keep praying we'll find Berto. Not just for Beth's sake. I can't stand the idea of his new business. How can someone do something so evil, Clint? I've been doing research on this at night. Do you know some of the horror stories about human trafficking? It breaks my heart. Some of these young women are even sold into by their families. I can't imagine." Clint pressed a kiss to the middle of her forehead.

"I know. You and I have probably read some of the

same articles. We're going to find him. The US and Mexican authorities have a joint task force on this. What's more, you, me, and Melvin are on the case." He tugged on one of her curls and she gave him a half-hearted smile.

"I can't make you feel better about this, can I?" he finally asked.

"Probably not. But seeing where you live. Finally meeting Mason in person, and his Sophia will help. I also really like the idea of Beth living close to us…"

"What?"

"It just seems like a lot. Let me up. I have to finish packing."

"What seems like a lot?"

"Well for one thing, where are Mama and Papa going to live? Thank God my grandparents will help them a little bit financially."

"Lydia, let's get one thing straight. They are your parents. I would also help them financially. As a matter of fact, we haven't talked about it, but I've already have something in the works.

Mason's dad is a contractor up in Portland and he's been working to find a fixer-upper. It's a duplex. I thought us each having our own space would be best, but it's a way to help them out until they can find a place of their own. I'm handy, and the team has said they would help out, so we should have it in great shape in no time."

The world stopped. She looked at the gray green eyes of her lover. This man she was going to marry. He turned shiny, then blurry. She wiped the tears out of her eyes.

"You didn't have to do that. I know how you must feel about my father."

"I thought about this a lot. I don't think I would have made the choices he made. But I understand a man who was trying to keep his family safe. He and I will be able to be neighbors."

She threw her arms around him.

After everything she had gone through in the last year, it was all worth it, because it brought her to this moment.

EPILOGUE

"Are you laughing at me again?"

"I don't know. Did you make me drive on Pacific Coast Highway even though the freeway would have taken half the time today?" Clint teased.

"I love that stretch of road."

What Lydia really loved was that Clint was back home.

Almost as soon as they moved into the small duplex in San Diego, he and his team mates shipped out for nine days. During those days she and her parents had time to get to know Jack Preston. Beth seemed to have flowered under his attention, but their time with Jack and Beth was too short. Berto was still out there and they had to leave. Lydia prayed she would see her little sister again soon. In the meantime, she savored the things she did have in her life.

She loved living in San Diego. Not only did she have her parents, but found herself immersed in a whole new family. Mason's fiancée Sophia, and her little brother Billy were absolute loves. They welcomed the Hidalgos with open arms. Sophia and Lydia bonded over a quart of

Baskin and Robbins ice cream the first night their men shipped off.

Sophia was surrounded by feisty senior citizens who even held card games. Her father was reluctant to join, but her mother had gone to the last one. But all of that was eclipsed by Clint being back.

"I missed you, Mr. Archer." Clint grabbed her hand and brought it up to his lips and kissed her palm.

"I missed you more, Miss Hidalgo." Lydia was sure they were wearing silly grins on their faces as they got out of Clint's truck. Tonight was a potluck for Tony and Frannie, two of Sophia's older friends.

"Are you sure we shouldn't have brought something for the potluck?" Lydia asked as they walked to the front door.

"Nah, they always have too much food. Frannie and Tony always cook a lot."

"Even for their own anniversary celebration? That doesn't make any sense."

"Hmmm, yeah, I guess that is weird, but they do like to cook. Wait 'til you try Tony's cannoli."

Sophia answered the door.

"Hello you two," she said giving Lydia a big hug. She winked at Clint over Lydia's shoulder. "People are in the backyard. Follow me."

Lydia stepped out into a wonderland. Above her head lights were suspended between the trees, and in the trees, there were tiny twinkling lights. Everywhere she looked the world glowed. They had outdone themselves for Tony and Frannie.

Clint guided her to the middle of the backyard where a small arbor was set up. There was a prettily decorated chair with a bouquet of red roses. She looked around for Frannie.

Music started, and a song from her childhood started to play. It was the one she told Clint always made her smile. It made her believe in miracles. She swayed a little as Louis Armstrong sang.

"Lydia Rose, take a seat."

"Clint?" He picked up the roses off the chair, and placed them in her arms, and guided her to sit.

"But Frannie–"

"I lied, this is your night." Clint brushed a soft kiss on her lips. She looked around, and everyone was standing around smiling at her. Her Mama was crying.

Oh God. Oh God.

Clint got gracefully down on one knee in front of her as Louis sang about red roses, sacred nights, and rainbows. This man who meant the world to her was holding a ring that outshone the stars in the sky.

"Lydia Rose, will you marry me?" She searched eyes the color of grass. She would never love anyone more than she loved Clint Archer.

She set aside the flowers, and sank to her knees, and held out her hand so that he could slip the ring onto her finger.

"To you Clint, my answer will always be yes. You're my hero."

"I love you Lydia, and you've got it wrong. You're the one who's the hero."

ABOUT THE AUTHOR

Caitlyn O'Leary is an avid reader and considers herself a fan first and an author second. She reads a wide variety of genres but finds herself going back to happily-ever-afters. Getting a chance to write, after years in corporate America, is a dream come true. She hopes her stories provide the kind of entertainment and escape she has found from some of her favorite authors.

As of winter 2018 she has fourteen books in her two best-selling Navy SEAL series; Midnight Delta and Black Dawn. What makes them special is their bond to one another, and the women they come to love.

She also writes a Paranormal series called the Found. It's been called a Military / Sci-Fi / Action-Adventure thrill ride. The characters have special abilities, that make them targets.

The books that launched her career, is a steamy and loving menage series called Fate Harbor. It focuses on a tight knit community in Fate Harbor Washington, who live, love and care for one another.

Her other two series are The Sisters and the Shadow Alliance. You will be seeing more for these series in 2018.

Keep up with Caitlyn O'Leary:

Facebook: tinyurl.com/nuhvey2
Twitter: @CaitlynOLearyNA
Pinterest: tinyurl.com/q36uohc
Goodreads: tinyurl.com/nqy66h7
Website: www.caitlynoleary.com
Email: caitlyn@caitlynoleary.com
Newsletter: http://bit.ly/1WIhRup
Instagram: http://bit.ly/29WaNIh

ALSO BY CAITLYN O'LEARY

The Midnight Delta Series

Her Vigilant Seal (Book #1)

Her Loyal Seal (Book #2)

Her Adoring Seal (Book #3)

Seal with a Kiss (Book #4)

Her Daring Seal (Book #5)

Her Fierce Seal (Book #6)

A Seals Vigilant Heart (Book #7)

Her Dominant Seal (Book #8)

Her Relentless Seal (Book #9)

Her Treasured Seal (Book #10)

The Found Series

Revealed (Book #1)

Forsaken (Book #2)

Healed (Book #3)

Shadows Alliance Series

Declan

Fate Harbor Series

Trusting Chance (Book #1)

Protecting Olivia (Book #2)

Claiming Kara (Book #3)

Isabella's Submission (Book #4)

Cherishing Brianna (Book #5)

Black Dawn Series

Her Steadfast Hero (Book #1)

Her Devoted Hero (Book #2)

Her Passionate Hero (Book #3)

Her Wicked Hero (Book #4)

Made in the USA
Coppell, TX
15 July 2021

58992040R00134